I0742717

A DEADLY AFFAIR IN THE PIRATE'S LAIR

Shiraz Jones Marine Rescue Mysteries
Book Two

Dedicated to the skipper and leaders of
1st Colerne Sea Scouts, who taught me Morse code.

Copyright

A Deadly Affair in the Pirate's Lair:
Shiraz Jones Marine Rescue Mysteries Book Two

ISBN: 978-0-6451187-8-0
Imprint: The Cozy Cabin Press
10 9 8 7 6 5 4 3 2 1

CONTENTS

Shiraz Jones Marine Rescue Mysteries are set in England and written by an English author.

Afternoon tea and crumpet, anyone?

6

CHAPTER ONE

Redcliff-upon-Sea, July 7th, 1789

"Hear ye, hear ye, hear ye. All rise for the Right Honourable Justice William Shackleton."

A stooped, elderly man shuffled into the court. He dragged long, black robes, and his white, powdered wig wobbled as he nodded to the court clerk. Bony fingers grasped the edge of a wooden lectern, and he pulled himself up one step at a time to an ornate, carved seat perched on a dais. His hooded, sunken eyes surveyed the court, as a schoolmaster might view a classroom of disobedient pupils.

His gaze settled on an unshaven man who wore an eye-patch. This man faced the centre of the court and stood squashed between two officials, his hands lashed with a rope.

"All sit," boomed the clerk. "The defendant alone shall remain standing for sentencing."

Justice William Shackleton sipped sherry from a small glass and cleared his throat.

"Thomas Blakey, you appear before me charged with manifold, heinous crimes. The court has heard how, together with your motley band of cut-throats, scoundrels and ruffians, you were responsible for the deaths of honest seafarers and the wrecking of well-founded craft. The appearance of your schooner on the horizon struck dread into the masters and crews of every law-abiding vessel. You committed brutal, unrestrained murder in the most barbaric way. Your despicable habit of disfiguring your victims by branding their chests with your initial has, without doubt, brought much vexation to those who grieve. For the last twenty years, your atrocities have been the scourge of the good citizens of Redcliff-upon-Sea, and I am determined to bring your abominable, wicked reign to its end."

A flicker of a smile passed across the defendant's face upon hearing the word 'reign'.

The judge paused and sipped again from the brown liquid in the glass next to his elbow.

"Thomas Blakey..."

The watching audience held its collective breath.

"For six counts on the charge of murder, four counts on the charge of shipwrecking, and a further two counts on the charge of piracy on the high seas, I sentence you to be hung by the neck until you are dead."

A mass gasp emanated from the public gallery, followed by cheers and hollers.

"Silence!" yelled the clerk. "Silence in court."

Justice William Shackleton extended his neck towards the defendant, snorted and spat generously. "Take him away. And may God forgive his wretched soul."

CHAPTER TWO

Present day

"Perishing picaroons, Shiraz, turn that phone screen off. You're destroying our night vision. As the skipper, I need to see where I'm going."

"Sorry, Murph. I knew we couldn't have cabin lights on at night; I didn't realise that rule applied to phones."

"The only lights we use inside the boat are dim, red ones," explained David, the qualified crewman. "No white lights on the boat after sundown. No torches, no phones, nothing that blinds us."

I felt my cheeks blush and hoped I could redeem myself. This was my third boat training session as a marine rescue volunteer, and my first after dark. I needed to prove to David how capable a crew member I was. Maybe even how good a date I'd be, if I could ever persuade him to look at me in that way. Although, I had started to wonder if he was too young for my thirty-eight years.

Redcliff Marine Rescue's vessel cruised out of the harbour mouth, and Murph steered a course directly between the red and green flashing lights marking the entrance. Besides Murph, David and me, on board was Emily, my new best friend, landlady and fellow trainee. She owned the Wicked Whelk café next door to the marine rescue station and was very useful in prompting me for the right answer when Murph asked one of his complicated questions. A girl has to employ all the resources available to her, right?

Murph grinned at me, and his teeth appeared amongst his bushy beard, spookily reflecting the red glow. "I could remind you, Shiraz, even though this is your first official night training, it isn't the first time you've been on the boat after dark, so I hope you've remembered something from that experience."

His subtle dig about the time he'd rescued Emily and me from West Cove beach when we'd misread the high tide needled me. I definitely needed to redeem myself.

"Of course I've remembered," I said. "We leave the green flashing light on our starboard side and the red flashing light on our port."

"Is that what we just did?" asked Murph.

I glanced over my shoulder as the boat headed away from the signals. "Um, no. They're the other way around."

Great. Way to make myself look stupider.

Emily piped up. "There's no red port left in the bottle."

"Why are you talking about alcohol?" I frowned at her. "After finishing that dodgy wine we found in your fridge last night, I don't want to think about it."

"It's a saying to help us remember which way around the lights are. When coming *in*, we leave the *red*, *port* light on the *left*. It's the opposite when exiting."

"Emily's right," said David, and I rolled my eyes, an action completely wasted in the dim cabin. "It's a useful mnemonic."

I repeated, 'No red port left in the bottle,' to myself a few times and determined to get it right on the way back. There was no way David could think Emily knew more than me. Even though she always did.

"Where are we heading tonight?" I asked Murph, hoping to deflect any more impossible questions.

"Blakey's Island. I'll show you the lights on the cardinal marks. It's very important for us to know which ones are which, so we never run aground." He pushed the throttles forward, and the vessel slop-slop-slopped over the waves.

"How far is it to the island? And why is it called Blakey's?"

"Blakey's Island's an outcrop of rock two miles off Redcliff," explained David. "You can see it clearly from shore."

"People have always called it Blakey's Island." Emily laughed. "It's strange, isn't it? We three have lived here all our lives and never questioned the history behind its name.

Then you, Shiraz, rock up in Redcliff, fresh from the city, and make us all curious."

Six weeks previously, during that odd, blurry period between Christmas and New Year, I'd marched out of my old London existence as the arm-candy of Monty Jones, the wealthy society PR guru. Gosh, you would've done the same, if you'd been in my situation. We'd been married eighteen years, since I began my so-called career as an aspiring model. I'd dutifully appeared alongside him in magazine photoshoots and on the red carpet. Every famous person knew Monty, and Monty knew every famous person. But there were three people in our relationship. Everybody knew he was engaged in an affair with his personal assistant, a scrawny young man named Darren.

Everybody except me. Stupid, innocent, trusting me.

And after I'd spent New Year's Eve locked in the bathroom, crouched in the foetal position under my Villeroy and Bosch, marble, gold-tapped sink, bawling my eyes out and realising I didn't have a single, genuine friend in the world who I could wail to, I'd wiped my eyes on a nearby Hampton and Astley pure-white towel, transferring streaks of black mascara and ruining it. Care factor? Zero. And I'd stood up, shook out my long, brown hair, inspected myself in the mirror and made a decision.

I, Shiraz Jones, was now an ex-society it-girl. My meaningless existence of cocktail parties with people I hated, photos in magazines of me at events I didn't give two hoots about and so-called friends who never called to ask if I was okay was over.

O. V. E. R.

History.

I'd selected my three favourite Burberry, Barbour and Salvatore Ferragamo coats, my four most prized Armani and Christian Dior dresses, five pairs of Ghost jeans and six pairs of shoes, including my treasured Gucci wedges. I'd stuffed tops, knickers, bras and a reasonable selection of jewellery into two expandable Louis Vuitton suitcases, grabbed my Hilde Palladino handbag, thrown my keys and my wedding ring down the sink incinerator, emptied our bank account and slammed the door of my city townhouse behind me.

No looking back.

I knew where I was headed.

The only place where I'd ever felt safe.

The only place where I'd ever felt comfortable.

The only place where I'd ever felt I was me. My childhood holiday town of Redcliff-upon-Sea, where I could forget about trying to impress people who didn't matter and make a fresh start with new, real friends.

People who knew nothing of my history.

People who'd never heard of Monty Jones PR, never heard of *Red Carpet Superstars* magazine and never heard of me. And during the phenomenally expensive New-Year's-Day-Quadruple-Rate-Thank-You-Very-Much-Madam taxi ride to the seaside town, my brain emptied of the horrible, vacuous thoughts which I'd realised shackled me to my old life.

Which recently purchased dress would I wear tonight? *New answer: Who gives a rats?*

Who, among Monty's clients, did I need to thrill today? *New answer: No one.*

What would the magazines print about me this week? *New answer: Nothing.*

As the gloomy outer London suburbs and grey asphalt motorway gave way to narrow, country lanes and green hedgerows, I sat forward and stared through the taxi's windscreen. And as soon as the first, exhilarating glimpse of the sea took me right back to the emotions of eight-year-old Shiraz on summer holidays with my parents and Poppy, my Corgi, an idea had bubbled to the surface.

How my new life could have meaning.

How I could make a difference and undertake something really worthwhile.

How the mention of the name 'Shiraz Jones' might command respect for my actions, not respect for which expensive designer my husband had clad me in that evening.

Which is how I came to be standing on the deck of Redcliff Volunteer Marine Rescue's boat at seven o'clock on a chilly, dark, winter's night asking why a lump of rock was called Blakey's Island.

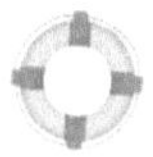

Murph pointed at the grey mass in front of us and switched on our vessel's powerful searchlight. We'd anchored off the island's small, sandy beach, backed by towering pinnacles of solid rock. Vegetation somehow clung to the base of the peaks, and it reminded me of the movie *Cast Away*.

"Blakey's Island," he announced. "Named after Thomas Blakey, a pirate who inhabited it over two hundred years ago."

"A pirate? In Redcliff?" I asked. "How romantic. Like something out of a Daphne Du Maurier book."

"He was a wrecker," continued Murph. "He and his band of merry men lured ships onto this rock, then, when they ran aground, he'd murder the crew and steal the cargo."

"Islands are normally named after famous people, aren't they?" asked David. "Not criminals."

Murph nodded. "Correct. Many times, the local council's proposed changing its name. For a few years, it was officially known as Puffin Rock, after the puffin birds which nest here. But nobody adopted the new name, and when the council themselves produced a tourist map with it clearly marked 'Blakey's Island,' they realised renaming it was a lost cause. Now it's a bird sanctuary, and no-one's allowed to land."

I peered along the beam of the searchlight which played across the beach, swaying with the motion of the boat. "Does anybody live on the island?" I asked.

"Years ago, a council warden inhabited a two-roomed hut at the rear of the beach, most recently a chap called Graham Woodhatch. But the council axed the funding for his role, and I can't imagine anyone's landed here since."

The rescue boat bobbed at anchor as we digested Murph's history lesson. Birds called in the dark, and a putrid, fishy smell wafted over from the beach. The rhythmic lap-lap-lap of the waves white-noised against the vessel's sides.

"Tours circling the island, together with the pirate story, would make a great tourist attraction," I said. "People from the city love all that stuff. Someone should start a business."

"Somebody already has," said Murph. "Jim Turner, a local boat owner, runs trips which he advertises as 'Fishing at Pirate Island.' His boat, the *Anstruther Pirate,* is decked out like a buccaneer's ship, he wears a patch over one eye, and he even flies the skull and crossbones. The pirate story's a secondary attraction to the fishing, of course. But his tours are very popular in season."

Murph switched off the spotlight, and Blakey's Island disappeared into the dark. I blinked, and dots of light danced as my eyes adjusted to the dim, red lights of the cabin.

"Let's remember why we're really here," he said. "It's pitch black. We're heading out of Redcliff on a shout. How do we make sure we don't run up on Blakey's Island?"

"Instruments?" I asked. "It shows up on the charts."

Murph covered the screen in front of him with his huge palm. "Now the instruments are broken. What do we do?"

"Um, navigate by the stars?" asked Emily.

"Can you do that?" said Murph. "If you can, congratulations. You're the only one of us. Have another guess."

Emily and I glanced at each other. I turned to Murph, shrugged and shook my head.

So much for impressing you and David tonight.

"Cardinal marks," said David. "There's a west cardinal mark at one end of Blakey's Island, and an east at the other."

"Shall we take a look?" asked Murph, and the chain's clatter-clatter heralded the raising of the anchor.

We motored gently around the island, which I couldn't see in the dark, though I could sense its looming presence. I can't explain this feeling, so trust me on this one. As we reached the end, a flashing light came into view.

"Count the flashes, Shiraz," said David.

"Three. Then it stops. Then three again."

"That's the east cardinal mark," said Murph. "The easiest way to remember how many flashes it makes is to think of a clock face. East is at three o'clock, so three flashes indicate safe water to my east. We must stay east of the light." He pushed the throttles forward, swung the wheel, and again I felt the island's proximity in the black, this time to my right.

"Here's the light at the other end of the island," said David. "It's a west cardinal mark, so how many flashes d'you think it makes?"

"Nine," said Emily. "Safe water to my west. I say goodnight to that light every evening from my bedroom window."

"Very good. And you're right. The west mark can be seen clearly from Redcliff."

Great. Emily goes to the top of the class. Time for me to show off.

"So a north cardinal mark would flash twelve times and a south cardinal mark six, right?"

I grinned at my powers of deduction.

"Nope," said David.

"You're kidding."

How will I impress you if my clearly correct answers are still wrong?

"A north cardinal mark flashes continually, and a south cardinal mark shows six short flashes, followed by one long," said Murph. "There aren't any north cardinal marks around Redcliff, but there is a south mark I can show you in Headland Bay another night."

We halted again on the north side of the island near the beach. My eyes had adjusted, and I discerned the difference in shades of grey between the sand and the rocks behind it.

"Murph, could we switch the searchlight on again? Shine it at the island? I think I saw something."

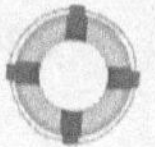

CHAPTER THREE

"You saw something?" repeated Murph. "Could you perhaps be a *little* more specific?"

"Sorry. I thought I saw a boat, pulled ashore amongst the trees."

"A boat in the trees? There can't be. The island's a nature reserve. It's out of bounds." He switched the spotlight on and turned our vessel, so it pointed directly at the beach.

"There! See?"

The beam swept across the stern of a rowing boat with a small outboard engine.

"Can you keep the light steady?" I asked Murph.

"Broadsided buccaneers, Shiraz. I'm trying. Unfortunately, the sea refuses to stay still."

"But you saw it, right?"

"I saw something. Everybody, eyes on where the searchlight's pointing."

The beam illuminated the island again.

"It looks like a tender," said David. "A small boat used to travel from the harbour wall to a yacht moored offshore. Someone's tied their tender to their buoy and taken their yacht for a sail, then the tender's come loose and drifted onto Blakey's Island."

The beam played across the wooden boat again. "Pass me the binoculars," called Emily. "There's a name written on its stern."

David tugged them from their packet and handed them to her.

"Stand by," said Murph. "I'll try to position the beam in the right place."

The light shone on the boat as Emily scanned the shore.

"It's hard to read while we're bobbing around. I think it says *Ruth*."

"*Ruth*?" I echoed. "I love the way people name boats after ladies."

"Yep," said Murph. "My parents owned a yacht called *Maud*. My dad spent his life explaining the pun."

"The pun?" asked Emily. "Oh, I get it. *Maud*. Moored."

We all laughed.

"It's almost nine o'clock," said Murph. "Enough training for one night. Let's return to base for a hot chocolate."

"I was getting chilly." I rubbed my hands together.

"And I brought cakes from the café that need to be eaten today," added Emily.

"Perfect," said David. "We'll ask around the harbour if any yacht called *Ruth*'s lost a tender, although it's not a boat name I recognise."

Emily shook her head at me the following morning in the Wicked Whelk café. "Shiraz, um, that looks very artistic, but how will we fit the tomatoes and cucumbers into the filled rolls if you've chopped them into cubes?"

I stepped back from the counter and inspected my handiwork. Cooking had never been my prowess; while married to Monty we'd always had a chef on staff, and I probably wasn't best placed to be Emily's kitchen hand. I began to wonder why I'd offered, but I needed to contribute something in return for staying with her in the apartment above the café.

"How d'you want me to chop them?" I asked, crossing my arms over my chest.

"Slice them thinly and evenly, like this." She snatched the knife from me and expertly slit a large tomato into ten precise, juicy discs, as if a slicing machine had suddenly materialised on the worktop.

"Oh. Sorry. When you said 'chop them up', I completely misunderstood. I'll start again." I swept my efforts into the compost.

"What are you doing?" Emily threw her arms in the air. "Don't throw them away. There's nothing wrong with them."

"You said I'd chopped them in the wrong shape. Make up your mind."

Emily sighed and placed an arm on my shoulder. "They're still edible. At worst, we could include them in a salad for dinner."

I held my palms up towards her. "Hey, don't assume I know anything about cooking. I'm doing my best."

"I know you are. Sorry I yelled. I've never met anyone who can't slice a tomato. No, don't pull them out of the green waste. You might find spiders in there."

She watched my attempts with the next vegetable carefully, and I realised I needed to divert her attention from my ineptitude. "What did you think of Murph's story about Thomas Blakey last night? D'you think it was true?"

"The rock must be called Blakey's Island for a reason. But all that stuff about pirates and shipwrecks; who knows how much of that's real? It happened over two hundred years ago."

"Someone thinks it's real. The chap who runs the fishing tours and flies the skull and crossbones."

"Jim Turner? Don't be daft. He's embellished the story for his own profits. Think about it. You're a mum or dad on a summer holiday in Redcliff, with small kids clamouring to go on a fishing trip. There are several boats in the harbour which'll take you out to drop a line and catch dinner. But what if one of the boats resembles a pirate ship, and the skipper's dressed like Captain Hook? And what if he promises a tour of Pirate Island while you're catching your mackerel? Which boat d'you think the kids will want to ride on?" She picked up my slices of tomato and arranged them on top of cheese and ham. "A little thinner, Shiraz? Try to get ten slices each, not four. I'll have to increase the price of sandwiches the way you're going."

I began to chop another tomato, and my knife slipped onto the board as I tried to follow her instructions. "You're right. Kids would love all that pirate stuff, whether or not the story's real. Have you taken his tour?"

"I haven't, but I know him. He comes into the café some mornings for a strong tea and a toasted bacon sandwich."

I put down the knife. "Shall we book his pirate cruise? For fun?"

"I'm not sure he runs them out of season. I'll ask next time I see him." She confiscated the knife and replaced it with a longer one. "Start on the cucumbers now, please. Sliced the same thickness as the tomatoes, if possible."

Three loud taps echoed from the café entrance.

I glanced over my shoulder. "Someone's at the door."

"We're closed on Sundays. But only one person knocks like that."

I rubbed a hole in the condensation and peered out. In the gloom of the winter's afternoon, I could see the back of a coat and a trilby hat. "Oscar," I said, and I opened the door. The arctic blast swept in a fit man of around seventy attached to a chocolate Labrador, who wasted no time in dragging his owner up to the counter.

"Cadbury, come away from there." Oscar jabbed his arm into the corner. "Sit. Stay." He turned to us. "Hello, Emily, hello Shiraz. I hope I'm not disturbing your labours."

"Not at all," I said. "I was helping Emily prepare food for the week."

"Helping may be an ambitious word." Emily laughed.

"Hey, I'm trying my best. What brings you here today, Mr Wainwright?"

"My wife's out at some church function, and Cadbury needed a walk, so I thought we'd stroll around the harbour. And then I wondered why the lights were on in the Wicked Whelk on a Sunday. I wanted to make sure it was you, and not someone robbing the café."

"Once a policeman, always a policeman?" I asked.

"I'm doing my bit for the community. Another of my bits for the community."

"Retired police sergeant, retired rescue skipper, volunteer Marine Rescue Gift Shop manager, Rotarian and local councillor," said Emily. "You should be decorated for services to the town. Arise, Sir Oscar, Knight of Redcliff-upon-Sea."

We all laughed.

"Don't forget, I'm the secretary of the Redcliff Icebergers Swimming Club too," he said.

"Did you swim this morning?" asked Emily.

"Every day of the year, five hundred yards."

"I didn't know Redcliff had a swimming pool," I said.

"Swimming pool?" Oscar swung his arm in a movement that encompassed most of the south coast. "Why would we need a swimming pool when we have the whole bay?"

"But it's February," I objected.

"We swim in the sea 365 days of the year, Shiraz. You should join us. We could do with some younger participants. Our average member's aged around 75."

"Um, no thanks. I might dip my toes in during the summer."

Oscar made a chicken-wing motion with his arms.

"Would you like a cup of tea?" asked Emily. "Shiraz and I were about to take a break."

"I wouldn't say no." Oscar sat at one of the café's tables and absent-mindedly laid his trilby on top of the salt and pepper shakers. Cadbury pricked up his ears as he heard Emily clattering crockery.

"Talking about the local council," said Oscar, "where d'you stand on this proposed development?"

"What development?" asked Emily. She arranged fruit buns on a plate and dumped them in front of him. I gave up trying to slice cucumbers evenly and sat opposite.

"I thought everyone knew about it," said Oscar. "The trouble with being on the council is you assume everybody reads the minutes of the meetings."

Emily brought a teapot and cups. She made a second journey with milk, butter and side plates. "Take a bun," she said. "They need eating."

Oscar poured tea, picked up a bun, ripped it open and spread a thick layer of butter. "The council's received an application to develop Blakey's Island. There'll be an article in the *Headland Bay Times* tomorrow. Their reporter interviewed the mayor yesterday."

"Develop it?" I asked. "I thought it was a bird sanctuary. What are they planning to build?"

"A city consortium's applied to construct a luxury, boutique hotel. I've seen the outline plans, and they show a modern, architectural structure which sits on one end of the island, embedded in the rock, protruding some distance into the sea. It's a horrendous edifice; looks like a supermarket car park on stilts."

"Who would want to stay there?" I asked. "Do they honestly believe people will pay to stay on a lump of rock?"

"This isn't the first island they've developed. I've studied their website, and they have similar monstrosities in the Caribbean, Greece, the Philippines and Australia. Their clientèle comprises film stars, industrialists, politicians, even members of royal families who want to get away from everything, especially nosy photographers."

"I understand the attraction of all the other locations you mentioned. Gosh, I've stayed on a private Caribbean island myself. They had security guards with guns, threatening any paparazzi who came too close. But why would a film star want to stay in Redcliff?"

"Hey," said Emily. "That's our home town you're referring to."

"Shiraz is right, though," said Oscar. "Redcliff's a lovely spot, especially in summer, but I agree; it doesn't compare with the Caribbean or Australia. Regardless, the company's submitted the initial application. A condition of being allowed to proceed to the next stage is a presentation to the public, followed by a vote. One of the company directors is in town next Wednesday to do exactly that."

"I have to say I'd be in favour," said Emily.

"Really?" I frowned at her. "You want all the bother and disruption?"

"Construction workers have to eat, Shiraz. It'd be great for the Wicked Whelk's off-season business."

"You'd be on the same side as half the council, then," said Oscar. "Five of us believe the injection of funds would benefit the town, and five of us believe it'll destroy it."

"And which side d'you sit on?" I asked him.

He gave me a stern look, then smiled to show he was joking. "If you'd known me for longer, Shiraz, that question would be superfluous." He thumped the table. "I'm one hundred per cent against it. Redcliff-upon-Sea's a unique, historic, harbour town with a fantastic sense of community, as you're discovering while volunteering with Marine Rescue. Our largest hotel's no more than a guest house. Why would anyone want a commercial operation such as this in our little town?"

"I agree," I said. "And Blakey's Island, with the pirate history, would be desecrated if it was developed."

"Pirate history?" Oscar puffed. "Hogwash. People like that chap Jim Turner will spin a romantic yarn, but Thomas Blakey was a common murderer, and it makes my blood boil when people make him out to be some kind of folk hero. That doesn't mean the island should be ruined, though."

"So what happens next?" asked Emily.

"The hotel company's director will present at the public meeting; we'll listen to what he has to say, then the council will vote on whether to allow the application to proceed to the next step."

I wrinkled my forehead. "From what you're saying, you're expecting a fifty-fifty split in the vote."

"Yes. The biggest supporter of the 'no' camp is the deputy mayor, Graham Woodhatch, a useful chap to have on my side. You might know him, Emily."

"He owns the fishing tackle shop in the High Street, and he used to be the island's warden?"

"Correct. He's a mad keen fisherman, and you'll find him out on his boat in all weathers. The mayor herself's the leader of the 'yes' voters, and I have my suspicions about her motives." He lowered his voice. "Last week, at church, she told my wife she's taking her family to Australia."

"I've always wanted to go there," said Emily. "Ever since I saw that movie *Priscilla, Queen of the Desert.*"

"I've been to Australia," I said. "Years ago, on a modelling shoot for Ray-Ban sunglasses. Has the mayor visited before?"

"She's never left this country, to my knowledge. And she intimated they'll be staying at an exclusive island resort. I'm wondering if she's being bribed."

"They're bribing the mayor? Ooh, scandal," said Emily. "I'd love to be a fly on the wall at that meeting. I hope the proposal goes through. Imagine all the construction workers buying coffees and toasted sandwiches every day. I could find a boat to deliver to the island. It'll be interesting to see how their plans take the nature reserve into consideration. Maybe the hotel can share the island with the puffins?"

"I'd caution against believing this will be good for the town," said Oscar. "These companies often bring in their own catering operations to feed their employees. But don't let me influence your thoughts. Come along to the meeting and decide for yourselves."

Emily turned to me. "Shall we go, Shiraz?"

"Seriously? Are you short of things to occupy your time?"

"I'll let you off more salad chopping."

My eyes lit up. "You've got a deal. We'll be there on Wednesday, Oscar."

"You and half the town, I reckon."

CHAPTER FOUR

"We should've come earlier." I surveyed the rows of chattering people, then swung my eyes to the rear of the auditorium where a gaggle of men and women stood against the walls.

"Yep. Standing room only," said Emily as we pushed into a gap. To our left, a long table with eleven chairs stood on a stage. Each place setting had a pad, pens and a glass of water. Behind the table, two large screens showed identical images of Redcliff-upon-Sea's council logo.

"Seven o'clock," said Emily, glancing at her phone. "Showtime."

Ten people entered via a side door and climbed steps to the stage. I spotted Oscar among them as they took their seats and tried to catch his eye, but he fixed his gaze on a spot in the distance. The woman who took the centre chair wore a chain around her neck with an ornate, gold medallion hanging from it, and I correctly identified her as the mayor. She checked her watch and whispered something to the man seated on her left. The place setting immediately to her right remained empty. She inspected her watch again, huffed, then stood and banged a wooden hammer dramatically. The crowds' murmurs quietened, while latecomers shuffled in.

"Welcome to Redcliff-upon-Sea Council's extraordinary February meeting," announced the mayor.

"Extraordinary's one way of describing it," shouted a man in the audience, and titters and giggles spread through the rows of seats.

I bent my head to Emily's ear. "Tough crowd tonight."

"Ssh."

The mayor continued. "This evening, we are very pleased to welcome Mr Jonathan Chadwick, of Chadwick-Mappin International Hotels."

A smattering of polite applause interspersed with muted booing emanated from the audience. The mayor sucked in a breath, then turned to a plump, red-cheeked man aged around forty, with a blonde fringe which he continually flicked out of his eyes. I could've sworn she fluttered her eyelashes at him.

"I do hope I have pronounced your name correctly, Mr Chadwick, or may I call you Jonathan?"

He smiled back and flashed teeth which appeared to have received recent investment from an expensive dentist. "Johnny's fine, now we know each other so well."

"Without further ado, may I invite Mr Johnny Chadwick to give us his presentation." She was now showing off her pronunciation, possibly even flirting with him. Johnny returned her bonhomie, stood, and adjusted his jacket which failed to reach around his tummy.

The image on the TVs changed to a company logo I hadn't seen before.

Johnny spread his arms wide. "Good evening, inhabitants of Redcliff-upon-Sea."

More applause and quiet booing.

"I'm Johnny Chadwick, Managing Director of Chadwick-Mappin International Hotels. I'm here to present our vision for the island which is known as Blakey's, located off your coast."

I was accustomed to privately educated schoolboys braying with their own self-importance, and I could see the audience remained unimpressed with his credentials.

"What about the nature reserve?" asked a middle-aged, blonde woman wearing a green jacket. She pointed her outstretched arm at the speaker.

"Our resort will share with the cute little birdies in perfect harmony," continued Johnny. "The proposed hotel is completely eco-friendly."

"Has anyone consulted the cute little birdies on this matter?" asked another man, to general laughter.

"There will be plenty of time for questions once Mr Chadwick has finished," said the mayor, banging her gavel. "Please be patient."

Johnny gave her a saccharine-sweet smile and planted his hands on his ample hips. He grinned at the audience like a second-hand car salesman.

"Chadwick-Mappin International Hotels will bring wealth and prosperity to the town of Redcliff." The image behind him now depicted male and female swimsuit-clad models, their teeth gleaming as they sat in designer bathing attire by a pool, sipping cocktails. I knew one of them and wondered if she'd given permission for her image to be used in the developer's marketing.

"Our existing hotels attract guests such as famous film stars, presidents, even members of the royal family." His presentation showed a group of foreign royals not in swimming attire and not sipping cocktails. I'd seen the same photo in *Red Carpet Superstars* magazine. Muttering spread through the crowd, and I could tell the picture had impressed them.

Johnny continued. "These exciting photographs show our existing resorts in other parts of the world." The display cycled through pictures similar to any I'd seen in luxury travel adverts: massive, infinity swimming pools, rooftop cocktail bars, bleached-white towels contorted into animal shapes on pristine, super-sized beds. I couldn't fathom how the company would plan to fit a resort of that size onto the outcrop known as Blakey's Island, but I'd only seen it close up after dark. Maybe it was larger than I thought?

A man in the audience echoed my thoughts. "How d'you plan to build a hotel like these"—he jabbed his finger at the screen—"on Blakey's Island? It's a lump of rock with a tiny beach. It doesn't have mains electricity or running water. This entire proposal's ridiculous."

A general hubbub indicated many of the audience agreed.

Johnny pulled himself up to his full height and full girth. "This will be the fifth island resort our company has constructed. Please, don't lose sleep over the finer details."

"Can we see the actual plans of what you propose in Redcliff, rather than a travel brochure?" asked another man.

Johnny's cheeks reddened. "The final plans are still in development. We've shown an outline to your council members."

"Well? Could you show us this outline?"

"The drawings are technical, and, unless you're all architects, probably not something you're used to comprehending."

I bent my head to Emily again. "That's a great way to alienate the entire audience. He's assuming, because they're mainly shopkeepers, farmers and fishing people, they're stupid."

Emily placed one finger on her lips. "Shh."

Johnny gesticulated dramatically as if he were a circus ringmaster. "We will release an artist's impression for all to peruse as soon as the current plans pass council."

"I've seen enough," said one woman. "What a waste of time." She stood and marched out.

"Me too." A man followed her, and several members of the audience copied him.

Johnny sat, and the mayor stood simultaneously. "Does anyone have any other questions for our guest, before the council votes on this proposal?" she asked.

"What's the point?" yelled an older man. "You've made your decision."

The audience nodded and murmured agreement, causing the mayor to bang her gavel again. She smiled at the guest speaker. "Thank you, Johnny. It's now time for the council to vote."

"Why don't *we* get a vote?" asked a man in the front row. He jabbed a finger at the mayor. "Have they paid you off?"

The mayor's cheeks turned the colour of pomegranates. She banged her hammer so hard, I thought its head might fly off. "All those in favour of allowing Chadwick-Mappin International Hotels' proposal to proceed to the next stage, please raise your hands."

Four hands rose among the council members seated behind the table. Johnny glanced around and jotted notes on a small pad.

"All those not in favour, raise your hands."

Oscar's hand shot up, followed by three others. Johnny again took notes.

The mayor stood, adjusted her glasses and addressed the room.

"The vote stands at four in favour and four against, with one abstention." She stared at the empty chair to her right. "I will therefore cast my deciding vote, which is to allow the proposal to go ahead to detailed planning. Motion carried five votes to four."

The audience chattered loudly, and the scraping of chairs and rustling of coats accompanied their heated conversation. Johnny grinned like a toothpaste advertisement. He and the mayor shook hands. She gave a tiny smile and raised her shoulders, as if they shared a secret.

"Time to go," said Emily.

I followed her through the departing throng into the winter's night.

Oscar joined us outside the council offices. He rubbed his hands together and blew on them. "Shocking," he said. "Absolutely shocking. That should never have been allowed to go ahead. Where on earth was Graham Woodhatch?"

"Was he the empty chair?" I asked.

"Yep, the deputy mayor. Not the most reliable of chaps, to be honest, but I can't believe he'd forget something as important as this. He's never missed a council meeting. Late, yes. Turns up in his fishing clothes smelling of pipe smoke, yes. A dreamer and a fantasist, yes. But to be completely absent, never. He loved Blakey's Island. Gosh, as the warden, he lived there for years and has the most personal connection to it of any of us. His 'no' vote would've stopped this in its tracks."

"This isn't the end, though?" I asked. "That meeting was to allow the proposal to go to the next stage. You can still stop it."

"Do we want to stop it?" asked Emily. "I quite like the idea of film stars and royalty holidaying in Redcliff."

"You may find the reality worse than the dream," I said. "They're not always the nicest company. I speak from experience."

"D'you want to come back for a cup of tea, Oscar?" asked Emily. "It's freezing out here, and we can chat in the warm."

"I'd love to, thanks. Then I must give Cadbury his evening walk. He'll be wondering where I am."

Hundreds of stars shone on this clear, moonless night as we strolled along the promenade. The waves rippled gently on the shingle to our left, and I stared at the horizon and tried to pick out the flashing white lights on either end of Blakey's Island. The cardinal marks, Murph had called them. I wondered if illuminations from the new resort would eclipse them. The soft, pink glow of the Wicked Whelk reflected in the sea by the harbour wall as Emily unlocked the apartment door, and we trudged up the stairs.

Oscar removed his coat and his trilby hat. "I can't understand where Graham Woodhatch could've been. If he'd attended the meeting, we would've been split fifty-fifty, and the motion wouldn't have passed. The council rules state we must have a majority."

"Have you tried ringing him?" I asked, as I filled the kettle and pressed the button to boil it. Boots, the Marine Rescue ginger cat, who spent most of his time asleep in Emily's living room, woke, stretched to his full three-feet length, stood and rubbed himself around my legs.

"Yes," said Oscar. "Directly before the meeting, as soon as I realised he was late. It went to voice mail."

Emily opened a plastic container and removed three cream finger buns oozing jam from their ends. I made tea, and we sat around her small, round dining table. Boots miaowed at full volume until Emily fingered cream into a bowl and placed it in front of him.

"That was a heated gathering, wasn't it?" I asked. "Are all council meetings like that?"

Oscar took a sip of tea and shook his head. "Nobody attends most council meetings apart from the councillors. I've never seen so many people."

"What's your opinion of Johnny Chadwick?"

"I know the type. Unlimited cash, and a spoilt brat used to getting his own way. If he can't get what he wants by legal means, he'll try illegal ones. I'm sure he and the mayor are colluding. His demeanour suggests he thinks this is a done deal."

"He's arrogant," I said. "He has a low opinion of the local opposition."

"Indeed," said Oscar. "When that gentleman asked to see the plans, and he insulted him by saying he wouldn't understand them..."

WEEEOOOOOO WEEEEOOOOOO WEEEOOOOOO

We all jumped at the wail of the marine rescue siren blaring from the building next door.

"Gosh," I said. "I wonder who needs rescuing at nine o'clock on a February night?"

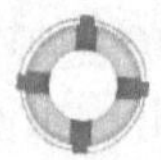

CHAPTER FIVE

We rushed to the window.

"When the alert goes off on a winter's night, it's usually serious," said Oscar. Nothing had happened yet, and the flashing red light which accompanied the siren lit up the harbour.

"I wish we were fully qualified, Emily, so we could go."

"Shiraz, I wake up at five o'clock to open the café. I am looking forward to going out on real rescues, but maybe not at this time in the evening."

"When I was a skipper, we didn't have a siren," said Oscar. "Instead, the dispatcher fired loud rockets into the sky, called maroons. One maroon meant: stand by, two maroons signified: proceed to the marine rescue station, and three maroons indicated we had a mayday situation requiring an immediate launch. These days, all the crew carry pagers. I miss the sound of the maroons."

"I remember the rockets," I said. "When I was a little girl on holiday here, I'd have my nose to the window as soon as I heard them. Then I'd stare out to sea and wait for the rescue boat to launch."

"Like we're doing now," said Emily. "Is it as exciting now you're an adult?"

"More so. I'll be doing this myself when I finish my training."

A white van screeched to a halt, and Murph stepped out and ran to unlock the marine rescue station, followed immediately by three other crew. The clatter of the roller door preceded the tractor's engine vibrating the night air, and we watched as it steered the trailer carrying the red rescue vessel down the launch ramp and into the water. Less than five minutes after they'd arrived at the station, the lights of the rescue boat penetrated the harbour entrance and disappeared into the night.

"I must be off," said Oscar. "Cadbury needs his evening walk. No doubt you'll let me know what tonight's rescue was about."

"Yep," I said. "I'll ask Murph if I see him tomorrow."

"I need to go to bed too," said Emily. "Goodnight, Oscar."

The door closed behind him, and I heard Emily brushing her teeth. I sat at the dining table and cradled my lukewarm tea. The story of Blakey's Island intrigued me. I'd loved playing at pirates as a girl on holiday here at Redcliff. There was even a photo somewhere of Poppy, my Corgi, wearing a cardboard pirate hat. Poor girl, she'd always had to be my playmate in the absence of any brothers and sisters. I'd read about wreckers and smugglers in children's books, but I hadn't realised they really existed.

"Emily?" I called.

"What? I'd just climbed into bed."

"Did you ask Jim Turner about his boat trips?"

"I haven't seen him."

"If he comes in tomorrow, could you ask him?"

"Okay. Goodnight."

"Goodnight."

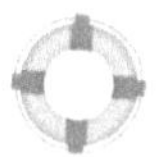

I woke with a start to the rhythmic banging of wind rattling my window. Interspersed with the gusts, somebody outside was clanging metal objects as if they were playing in a poorly rehearsed steel band. After I'd sat up and rubbed my eyes, my phone advised me I'd severely overslept, and it was 10:15. Whoops. I threw the covers off and hoped Emily was coping fine by herself in the Wicked Whelk. She was probably coping better without my contribution, to be honest.

The view, once I'd pulled my curtain back, showed a ferocious sea crashing over the harbour wall with grey clouds scudding across an angry sky. I couldn't see who made the noise outside my bedroom, so I tugged on jeans and a jumper and purloined Emily's sheepskin coat. Time for my morning double shot, skinny latte. The first of the day, therefore the best.

Murph knelt in the shed beside the rescue vessel, wearing a black visor that made him look like a medieval knight about to go into battle.

"Morning, Shiraz," he said. "Cover your eyes from the welding torch while I touch up this last joint."

I shielded my face and looked away as his tool fizzed and crackled.

"All done." Murph removed the visor and packed away his apparatus. "We damaged the spotlight mount in the rescue last night. Thankfully, we can fix that quickly without taking the boat out of service."

"What was the shout?"

"A mystery," said Murph. "The Coastguard received a call from someone saying her husband had gone fishing last night and hadn't returned. Apparently, he wasn't the most reliable chap, and he was often late home, but this time, he was really late. He'd missed dinner and an important meeting he was supposed to be attending, so she was naturally anxious."

"She would've been. Did you find him?"

"We found his boat." Murph pointed at a small, white vessel with a half cabin, pulled up on the shingle inside the harbour. The sides and bottom were discoloured from being in the water. "Adrift and unmanned, close to Blakey's Island. Very odd, considering the calm northerly wind. I could understand someone falling overboard in the south-westerly gale today but, last night, it was a millpond."

"So where's the fisherman?"

"That's a good question. Together with the Coastguard helicopter and a rescue boat from Headland Bay, we searched until midnight, but finding a person in the water's hard enough during the day, let alone in the dark. If he'd fallen overboard, even with a lifejacket on, he'd have lived an hour at most. The sea temperature in February's eight degrees centigrade."

"How come the Coastguard haven't tasked us to look for his body this morning?" I watched for his reaction at my use of the word 'us', even though I knew he wouldn't allow me to join a real search yet.

"In these conditions?" He pointed at the spray saturating the harbour footpath. "If he's been in the water all night, he won't be alive. And we can't risk becoming casualties ourselves. Coastguard teams are searching the shoreline, but it's too windy today for us or the helicopter."

"Did you know the missing person, Murph?"

"Only to say hello to. He runs the fishing tackle shop. A man called Graham Woodhatch."

My heart paused briefly. "The chap who used to be the island's warden? He's now the deputy mayor?"

"That's the one. D'you know him?"

"I don't but, if you'll excuse me, I need to see someone who does."

DING DONG

A confusion of deep barks and yells followed my ring at Oscar's doorbell.

"Coming, coming. Quiet, Cadbury. Quiet! In your bed."

Oscar swung the door open dressed in old clothes, and I correctly guessed gardening was on the agenda this morning. "Shiraz, hello," he said. "What brings you here this morning? You look out of breath. Come in."

He led me along the hall into the kitchen.

"I ran from the marine rescue station. I know why the deputy mayor wasn't at the meeting last night. I know what happened to him."

"Woah. Take your time." Oscar frowned and looked at me sideways as I held onto the back of a seat and panted.

"He was out on his fishing craft yesterday," I said between puffs, "but he didn't come home. Murph told me the shout last night was to Graham's boat. They found it adrift and abandoned off Blakey's Island. Together with the Coastguard helicopter, they searched until midnight, but they didn't find any sign of Graham in the water. And the

Coastguard hasn't asked Redcliff Marine Rescue to recommence the search again this morning, because…"

"…it's too rough." Oscar completed my sentence. "Sorry to have drawn that out of you, but I wanted to make sure we'd both received the same information. The mayor called shortly before you arrived and informed me the police spoke to her earlier this morning, after they'd told his wife. He can't be alive, tragically. There's no way anyone would survive a tumble overboard in February."

"That's terrible," I said. "I didn't know him, but no one deserves to drown alone at night in a freezing sea."

I sat down heavily on one of Oscar's kitchen chairs.

"Would you like a drink?" Oscar waggled a mug at me.

"I was on my way to pick up a coffee from the Wicked Whelk when the conversation with Murph delayed me." I looked up at him. "I haven't reached the coffee part of my morning yet."

"Come on," said Oscar. "Let's both go down to the café. I'll buy; you always say you can't function in the morning without your triple shot whatever."

You're not wrong there. I'm lucky my jumper's on the right way around.

"Thank you. We can tell Emily what we've discovered. If she hasn't heard on the grapevine."

"Yep. You can't keep a lid on important news for long in this town." Oscar swiped Cadbury's lead from a hook, at which the chocolate Labrador jumped up and sat at his feet. With the lead clipped to his collar, Cadbury trotted along beside us.

"I'll tie him outside the café while we have our drinks," said Oscar. He addressed the dog. "You're not allowed in the Wicked Whelk during opening hours, are you, Cadbury?"

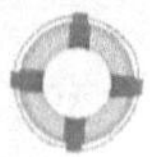

CHAPTER SIX

Anthony Blakey inspected himself in his full-length mirror. He'd always been a perfectionist, and his immaculately ironed shirt and creased-in-the-right-places suit showed he was a man who meant business.

Serious, important business.

The deal with the nature reserve's ex-warden.

The vote to allow the hotel proposal to proceed.

The matter of the little boat, and the man's disappearance, which hadn't met with his approval.

These matters paled into insignificance, as an image of Shiraz retained podium position in his mind.

He knew her.

He knew her history.

And he knew her future.

And one day, she'd know it too.

But not yet.

Not today. Today was merely a milestone on their journey.

He minutely adjusted one cufflink, imperceptibly straightened his tie and checked the time on his Rolex watch.

10:00 a.m.

Thirty minutes.

Thirty minutes until his train departed.

All his preparations were complete.

All the loose ends tied up.

His lawyer had dealt with the last-minute hitch involving those idiots in the police.

He lifted the handle of the unwieldy packing case and silently thanked his decision to mount two castors on one end.

The door to his London apartment clicked closed, and he trundled the heavy box towards the elevator.

Button 'G'.

Ground floor.

The second phase of his plan began now.

CHAPTER SEVEN

"Drowned?" said Emily, in a hushed voice across the counter. "Graham Woodhatch?"

"That's what it sounds like, although they haven't found a body yet." I glanced over my shoulder. Most of the early customers had left the Wicked Whelk, and the café was in the mid-morning lull before lunch service.

"Gosh. Wow. I don't know what to say. How d'you know?"

"Oscar received a call this morning. Murph was out last night looking for the poor man; they found his boat adrift. But he wasn't in it."

"Where?"

"A short distance off Blakey's Island. Um, could we order? I haven't had my morning coffee fix yet."

"Sorry, yes, of course. Double shot skinny latte? And a strong Earl Grey tea, no milk for you, Oscar?"

"As usual." Oscar pulled a banknote from his wallet. "We'll sit at the table in the corner." He hung his coat on the back of a chair and placed his hat on the table.

"I can't believe it," said Emily, almost to herself, while the coffee machine sputtered and hissed. "Graham Woodhatch. Drowned."

My fingers tapped on the counter in caffeine-desperation, and I rested my other hand on them to calm them down. I didn't want to appear rude, did I?

"Did you know him well?" I asked, watching Emily's hands prepare my drink as intently as a hopeful dog sitting beside its mistress on speak night.

She tapped the milk jug gently. "I only knew him as a customer. He came in for a weak cappuccino and a toasted sandwich before a fishing trip."

I grinned at her propensity for identifying people by their coffee orders, then realised grinning wasn't entirely appropriate in the circumstances and quickly altered my expression to a suitably serious one.

"But he wasn't one of the commercial fishing community," she continued. "His shop sold hobby fishing gear, rods and lines, that kind of thing." She shook her head and puffed. "Here's your coffee and Oscar's tea. I'll join you in a minute as soon as I've served these other customers."

I took a quick sip of double shot heaven to steady my hands before carrying the cups to the table. In his capacity as husband-in-charge-of-public-appearances, Monty had always nagged me about my coffee habit, but no matter how hard I tried, I hadn't been able to break it. And nor had new me. New Shiraz; old Shiraz—both of us suffered identical caffeine addiction.

"Thank you," said Oscar, as I placed his steaming cup in front of him. He leant towards me. "Recap what Murph told you. I want to digest it fully."

I sipped and licked froth mixed with chocolate sprinkles from my lips. The lack of lipstick-taste reminded me I'd left the house without looking in the mirror. I tossed my hair and hoped it wasn't a complete bird's nest. "The Coastguard called out Marine Rescue last night to search for a missing fisherman. His wife reported him absent from dinner. She wasn't overly concerned because he was often late but, as we know, he missed the council meeting."

"With potentially catastrophic consequences," said Oscar. "The town gossip mill's on full power following the vote."

Emily placed her hot chocolate on the table and sat beside me. "What's the gossip?" she asked.

"I was referring to chatter following the vote to permit the hotel development to move to the next stage," said Oscar. "But Shiraz was telling us about last night's shout."

"Murph and his crew launched at nine o'clock to search for Graham," I continued. "The Coastguard helicopter was involved, and Headland Bay Marine Rescue too, but Murph said searching in the dark's impossible."

"He's not wrong," said Oscar. "I can't remember any night search I've been involved with which had a good outcome."

"They found his boat," I said. "Abandoned and adrift off Blakey's Island. They towed it back here."

"I'd like to inspect it," said Oscar. "None of this makes sense. Graham Woodhatch fished off that boat in all weathers. He was an experienced fisherman, and an expert boater. He would've been out in conditions far worse than last night's gentle breeze. And, as the only person I know to have lived on Blakey's Island, he would've been familiar with the tides and currents. Where on earth is he? I can't believe someone like Graham would've fallen overboard." Oscar frowned and studied the ceiling briefly.

Emily and I both glanced upward to see what he was looking at, but then he lowered his gaze. "You two will say this is my ex-policeman's mind working overtime, but I think there might be more to this story than an angler tumbling from his craft."

"Ooh," exclaimed Emily. "What d'you suspect?" She leant towards Oscar.

"Let's not jump to any conclusions. But I would like to inspect his boat."

"Do you think he's definitely dead?"

"I hate to say it, but I'm sure. Recap. What do we know? He went on a fishing trip, an activity very familiar to him. Some hours later, the Coastguard received a call from his wife, saying not only was he late home, but he'd missed the council meeting. They tasked various assets to search for him and found his boat adrift near Blakey's Island with no one on board. After looking for him in the water until midnight, the hunt was called off, and they towed his unmanned boat back to harbour. This morning, these high winds make continuing the search impossible."

"Now what?" I asked.

"Now, either his body washes up on shore, or it doesn't."

"Is anyone searching the shore?" asked Emily. "In case his, um, body, appears. Gosh, I don't feel comfortable speaking about a body when we don't know for certain he's dead."

"Yes." I nodded. "Murph told me Coastguard teams are combing the beaches."

"The sea doesn't always give away its secrets," said Oscar. "Sadly, some people are never found."

Oscar held the café door for me and unclipped Cadbury from the ring in the wall outside the Wicked Whelk. He trotted alongside us past the marine rescue building towards the harbour, pausing only to inspect the base of a lamppost. The gusts of wind blew my hair horizontally, and I wished I'd tied it up.

"Ah," I said. "We may not be able to have as close a look as we'd like."

Graham's boat still lay where Murph had showed me, on the beach alongside the rescue boat launch ramp. Blue-and-white tape flapped in the wind with the words 'Police Line—Do Not Cross' emblazoned along it, blocking our proposed inspection. A stout, middle-aged officer guarded the beached craft.

"Bert?" I asked, as I approached him. "What's going on? Why is Graham Woodhatch's boat cordoned off?"

"Morning, Miss Shiraz," said Bert. He nodded at Oscar. "Precautions. Sarge asked me to keep the public away until we'd completed our analysis of the vessel."

"Do you suspect foul play?" asked Oscar. "Didn't he fall overboard?"

"I couldn't possibly comment," said Bert. "Nothing's been publicly released yet."

Oscar peered across the tape at the boat and slitted his eyes, then subtly waved to me, pointed his finger at Bert with one hand and made a mouth opening and closing action with the other.

I knew exactly what this meant.

"Isn't this weather bracing, Bert?" I said.

"Indeed. I'm glad to have my thick coat on today. I could've done with one of Miss Emily's hot pies to warm up my insides."

I loved Bert's soft, local accent and could listen to his relaxing tones all day.

"Yesterday," he continued, "you could almost feel spring in the air. Whenever we get these sunny days in late winter, the temperature climbs a few degrees, the daffodils start opening, and people emerge from hibernation. Why, I was only saying to the wife last night, we're planting out our spring vegetables earlier and earlier each year. Must be this global warming business."

From the corner of my eye, I noticed Oscar remove a tennis ball from his pocket and gently roll it under the police tape. Cadbury sprinted after it and clomped it in his jaws before it reached the boat. He ran back to drop it at Oscar's feet and sat, waiting for it to be thrown again. What on earth were they doing?

"Yes," said Bert, "I told her it wouldn't last. As soon as this south-westerly swings around, we'll be back to frosts at night, mark my words."

I spied Oscar throwing the ball again, and Cadbury retrieving it. I knew he was up to something, although I didn't know what. My job was to keep the policeman distracted.

"Gosh, yes," I said. "The wind makes my window rattle. It keeps me awake. But I enjoy feeling all warm and cosy while the gale's blowing outside."

"Cadbury, now look what you've done." Oscar yelled at the dog, who put his head on one side and gave his master a puzzled look. "You've got your ball stuck under that boat. Now I'll have to pull it out for you." He turned to the officer. "Sorry, Bert. Could I nip under the tape to grab Cadbury's ball? I don't know how the silly animal wedged it under there."

"You're not supposed to cross a police barrier," said Bert, but it was too late. Oscar had lifted the police tape and marched towards the boat, as Cadbury pawed at the ball stuck under it.

"Quick as you can," said Bert. "Sarge won't like it if he sees you there."

This was another distraction cue. "Bert, whose boat is that moored against the harbour wall?" I pointed. "The one with the black flag at the top of the mast."

Bert followed my finger. "That's Jim Turner's boat, the *Anstruther Pirate*. The flag's the skull and crossbones. He runs local fishing trips with a pirate theme, taking daytrippers out to Blakey's Island and telling them tales about the smugglers and wreckers who operated here."

"Pirate theme? Were there pirates here?"

"Of course there were, Miss. Redcliff's well known as a buccaneer's haven. Mind you, that was a long time ago. There haven't been pirates around here since the 1700s."

"Got it," called Oscar, holding up the yellow tennis ball before replacing it in his pocket, much to the dismay of Cadbury. He lifted the police tape and ducked back under.

"Right, Shiraz. We mustn't detain Constable Bert from his important work any longer. Shall we take a breezy stroll along the seafront?"

"That'd be lovely," I said. "Goodbye, Bert. Will you be relieved of guard duty soon?"

Bert looked at his watch. "Constable Lachlan's coming in an hour. Just in time for me to pop into Emily's café for a tea and a pastry before she closes. I hope she has the chocolate-filled flavour today."

"I'm sure she has. She made fresh ones this morning."

"Wonderful. Good day to you."

Cadbury tugged Oscar away, and I walked on the other side of him. "What was that about, with Cadbury's ball?" I asked. "You did that on purpose, didn't you?"

"You're a perceptive young woman, Shiraz. And thank you for keeping Bert busy. I wanted to have a closer look at Graham Woodhatch's boat, and that was the only way I could think of doing it."

"What were you looking for?"

"Anything different. Anything that shouldn't be there. Anything suspicious."

"And did you find something?"

"No, but while I was retrieving Cadbury's ball, I snapped photos with my phone. We'll have a look at them later on a bigger screen."

"Well done. D'you think the police suspect there was more to this than Graham falling from his boat?"

"I don't know what the police suspect, but I know what I believe. This wasn't an accident."

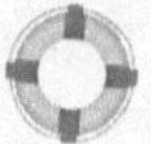

CHAPTER EIGHT

Anthony Blakey stared from the window of his first-class train carriage, while the handles on the wooden crate stencilled 'A Blakey' rattled in the goods wagon behind him.

The train scythed through small towns, parting the brown, barren fields as they awaited the green shoots of spring to poke through.

He knew nothing of farm work, of the effect of the seasons on the crop, of the tough labours the country man and woman endured.

A lifelong city dweller, he'd never lived in a street with gaps between its buildings, and his anxiety at what he might find in rural Redcliff-upon-Sea gnawed at his mind.

The anxiety of never being in her presence again prickled him more.

Two months since he'd last seen her.

Eight weeks.

Fifty-three days, ten hours and forty-seven minutes.

She'd vanished.

One minute, she posed at every function, featured in every gossip column, centrefolded every society magazine: Shiraz Jones, doyen of the society merry-go-round.

The next minute, she'd gone.

Gone, as if she'd never existed.

The paparazzi moved onto another front-cover candidate, and Shiraz, erstwhile wife and constant partner of Monty Jones, PR guru to the stars, had disappeared like dandelion seed in the breeze.

Pooof.

And then...

Then he'd found her.

Found her where no one could've ever predicted.

A tiny snippet he'd read idly over his Sunday morning coffee, in his habitual city coffee shop.

An article he hadn't really been interested in.

An article about marine rescue, a subject that few people in London cared about.

A black-and-white, grainy photograph of a building with a rescue boat on a trailer.

Three people posing in front of it.

And the caption: "Coxswain Brian Murphy with two of Redcliff Marine Rescue's newest recruits, Shiraz Jones and Emily Philpot."

As unlikely as her new situation seemed, there couldn't be more than one Shiraz Jones in the country.

Could there?

Then, a second stroke of luck. A chance remark overheard at a society party. A party where, in the good old days, he might've glimpsed her. Followed her every move. Maybe even brushed past her.

He'd tuned out of the group conversation between property developer acquaintances discussing a potential new hotel site, when one of them had clearly said the word 'Redcliff'. Directly, his eyes focussed on that man like sniper's laser beams.

"I'm sorry," said Anthony. "Did you say Redcliff?"

"I did," said the middle-aged developer, a portly man called Johnny who'd had far too much to drink and would rely on the young blonde limpeted to his side to call them a taxi later. "Redcliff-upon-Sea? D'you know it?"

"Um, I know of it. What are you planning there?"

"Another island resort for this lot." Johnny swept his blazered arm around in a circle at the other well-heeled guests and liberally spilt his Aperol Spritz over the carpet. "But this one's going to be local. Somewhere they can escape for a night or three without boarding a plane."

"Interesting. An island?" Anthony tried to conceal his eagerness to hear more. Maybe Shiraz was involved with this developer? That was why she was in Redcliff, perhaps?

"An island two miles off Redcliff's coast," explained Johnny. "It's a nature reserve for seabirds now, but that kind of detail's never bothered us in the past. The town itself's a backwater full of country bumpkins, but we'll build a helipad so none of the guests need encounter the locals." He looked around for laughter, and the blonde rewarded him by throwing her head back and braying. "Plus, we've got the mayor in our pocket. She thinks she's earnt herself a fortune, but it's small change to us."

"How will you finance it?" asked Anthony. Maybe Shiraz's contacts were involved with that side? Sleeping partners.

"The same as the other resorts. An international consortium. I'm one of several investors on the board."

"The whole region's so romantic," the blonde chimed in. "Johnny's island used to belong to a pirate who captured ships, stole treasure and murdered the captains. Johnny's going to make it a luxury resort with a *Pirates of the Caribbean* stage show, and I'm going to be the star, aren't I, darling?"

"Of course you are," said Johnny. "You'll be absolutely fabulous." He squeezed her so hard her eyes seemed to bulge, and the polished, bleached-white grin never left her face.

Anthony smiled back, as the first inklings of a plan formed in his mind.

The sleepy seaside town of Redcliff-upon-Sea was about to become re-acquainted with its violent past.

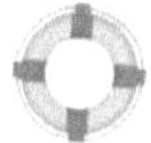

CHAPTER NINE

Oscar, Emily and I sat around the television in her apartment that afternoon. A plate of leftover cakes from the café rested on a table between us, and we began the silent negotiation which occurs when everybody really wants the moist, brown one with the chocolate icing, but nobody's brave enough to claim it.

Emily held out her hand. "Pass me your phone, Oscar, and we'll connect it to my TV and look at the photos."

"Here you go. It's an old one, but it still works fine. My son gave it to me when he upgraded to one of those fancy new ones with the folding screen."

She studied the base of the phone, peered inside a shoebox beside her and shook her head. "Why is it, when you put several cords into a box, they magically tangle themselves into knots during the night? This is ridiculous." She held up a ball of black-and-white leads which reminded me of my grandmother's knitting before she made it into a scarf. Boots eyed the end of one wire dragging along the floor and pounced on it before it could escape.

"I've cables for my tablet, cables for my phone and weird cables which don't seem to fit anything. But none of them go into Oscar's device. Doesn't the 'U' of USB stand for 'universal'?"

Boots jumped on the ball of cords and fought with it briefly before he decided it wasn't worth the effort and stopped for an emergency paw lick.

"Boots." Emily threw her arms in the air. "You're not helping."

I took Oscar's phone from her and inspected it. "D'you own a Kindle?"

"Yes. Why?"

"I think this uses the same type of charger."

"It's beside my bed," said Emily. "I'll fetch it."

She returned with her Kindle cable, and we successfully connected Oscar's phone to her television. Oscar browsed through his photos and, after we'd viewed Cadbury on the beach, Cadbury in the park and Cadbury on the clifftop walk, the pictures he'd surreptitiously taken that morning of Graham's craft appeared.

"You should've seen Oscar's subterfuge," I said to Emily. "He threw Cadbury's ball for him so that it became stuck under the side of Graham Woodhatch's fishing boat. That gave him an excuse to duck under the police tape and snap these photos."

"I hope Bert didn't realise what I was really up to," said Oscar.

"Definitely not. He was too busy talking about the weather and Emily's pastries." I inspected the first image, which showed the boat's underside. "D'you see anything out of the ordinary, Oscar?"

Oscar leant forward and peered at the screen. "All I see is a boat which needs the weeds and barnacles scrubbed off its bottom. Which is exactly what you'd expect, because that's what it is." He flicked to the next photo. "This shows the bow of the vessel. I can't notice anything untoward there, can you?"

"I'm no expert," said Emily, "but it looks like a normal boat."

"Exactly." He swiped the phone again. "The third photo shows the stern. I couldn't get a good angle, for fear Bert would work out what I was up to, but the engine seems fine. No clues there. You can clearly see the waterline in the brown stain around the hull. If someone else showed me this photo and asked me what it was, I'd simply say it's a small fishing boat which is usually kept in the water. Nothing odd."

"D'you have any other pictures?" I asked.

"There's one of the inside. I had to take it quickly, so I'm afraid it's blurred." Oscar swiped forward to an out-of-focus shot of the interior of the boat. We could see the shape of the wheel, two seats and a black rectangle mounted in front of them, which we concluded was the instrument panel.

"It's not the best photo," said Oscar, "but again, I see nothing unusual. This makes no sense at all. What happened to Graham?"

I leant forward and squinted at the blurry image. "There is something unusual I've noticed."

"What?" said Emily and Oscar together.

"Graham was a keen fisherman, right?"

"Obsessed," said Oscar. "He lived and breathed fishing. Goodness knows who'll run his angling business now."

I pointed at the picture on the screen. "D'you notice anything missing?" I asked. "Where's all his fishing gear?"

Oscar's eyes darted around the photo of Graham's boat. "You're right, Shiraz. There's no sign of any fishing tackle. No rods, no nets, none of the usual paraphernalia fishing people accumulate. And I know Graham accumulated a lot. He loved to receive deliveries of new stock at the shop so he could take samples and test them. But his boat's completely empty." He raised both eyebrows and puffed out his cheeks. "None of this makes any sense at all. Maybe Murph removed the gear when he'd rescued the boat?"

"I can ask him," I said. "But why would he do that?"

"Could it be Graham was never in the boat?" asked Emily. "The boat came loose from its moorings and drifted out to sea without him?"

"No. It was a gentle northerly wind yesterday evening. Not like this howling south-westerly. A northerly wind means, if his boat had come loose from its mooring, it would've blown further into the harbour."

"Gosh," said Oscar. "You've been a marine rescue volunteer in Redcliff for six weeks, and you're already explaining the effects of wind direction. Well done."

I blushed and glanced down.

Oscar looked at Emily and me. "Also, if Graham's boat had drifted off by itself, why wasn't he at the council meeting? I'm sure Graham was aboard his boat last night. But where on earth is he now?"

"What do the police think?" asked Emily.

"I don't know," said Oscar, "but they've roped off his boat and made it a crime scene."

"Crime scene? Do they think someone killed him?"

"It's standard procedure in the case of a missing person. If the vessel contains any evidence, they don't want random members of the public trampling over it."

"Or ex-policemen playing ball with their dog?" I gave Oscar a knowing grin.

"Who wants to guess what happened to him?" Emily grabbed a pad and pen. "Shiraz?"

"Hang on." I shook my head at her. "Let's not get involved with another investigation. I've never met this Graham Woodhatch chap, and while I'm sorry for his family that he's missing, I don't see I can offer anything to find him."

"You're being modest," said Oscar. "You have such an investigative mind, and once you're in full flow, you leave no stone unturned. I could've done with someone like you on the force when I was the sergeant here."

"That's very flattering, but I wouldn't know where to start with a man missing at sea."

"We're members of Redcliff Marine Rescue," said Emily. "We're more familiar with the water than the average person in the street. Look how you knew about the wind direction, and where his boat would've ended up."

"Yes, but that doesn't mean I can find missing persons. And you have more knowledge about marine rescue facts. You're the one who gets the answers to Murph's questions right when I can't."

"I study books and memorise them. Your strength is analysis: working things out, rather than regurgitating words you've remembered. I can't do what you do."

"You make a great team," said Oscar. "Each of you has skills that complement the other. And, Shiraz, this all ties in with the pirate story you're interested in."

"How?"

"It's about Blakey's Island. Graham Woodhatch was the island's warden and was very keen to prevent it being developed into a private resort. He loved the wildlife and the peace of the nature reserve."

"And Murph found his boat adrift off the island," said Emily. "I'm seeing a lot of connections here."

"I don't want to see Blakey's Island turned into a hotel either," I said. "I don't think the puffins would want to share their home with film stars. But even if we try to work out what happened to Graham, how would that change anything?"

"Because in the unlikely event he turns up alive," said Oscar, "the next round of voting will be split fifty-fifty, so the hotel proposal won't be a done deal."

"Unless someone changes their point of view."

"Yes, and I'm sure there'll be subtle campaigns to influence the council."

"Is that legal?"

"If you gave a councillor a direct bribe, no. But there's nothing to stop anyone lobbying."

The sound of the rock band AC/DC playing 'Thunderstruck' blasted from Oscar's phone.

"I wish I knew how to change that ring tone," he said, pressing the green button. "Hello?"

Pause.

"Yes, this is Oscar. Have they? Where? And do they definitely know it's…?"

We heard a female voice speaking into his ear but couldn't discern the words.

"I see," continued Oscar into the phone. "Tragic, absolutely tragic. All right. Thanks for letting me know. Bye."

He pressed 'end' on the Nokia, sighed and shook his head.

"Who was that?" asked Emily.

"The mayor." Oscar looked up. "The Coastguard shore team found a body at East Beach. Very bloated and smashed up."

"That's awful," I said, pushing my plate to one side. "I don't feel hungry anymore." Boots had no such scruples and used my lap as a step to leap onto the table. Before I could stop him, he tugged the ham from my bread roll, jumped down and sat in the corner chewing it.

Emily clonked her plate on the table. "Is it Graham?"

"They haven't positively identified the body yet. But it has to be, doesn't it? The chances of two people falling into the water and drowning on Wednesday night are infinitesimally remote."

"When did they find him?" I asked.

"This morning. The south-westerly storm must've washed him to shore."

"And smashed him on the rocks," said Emily. "What a horrible, horrible thing. The sea has no respect for the dead. Did the mayor say anything else?"

"Yes. She told me his widow's totally distraught."

"She would be, poor woman. Is someone looking after her?"

"Friends, probably. They don't have any family, so far as I know. She has a large friendship group through her membership of Redcliff Amateur Dramatic Association." He pinched his lips together and squeezed his eyes shut.

"Did you know him well, Oscar?" I held his arm.

"Yes, from being colleagues on the council. Graham was one of the good guys. Disorganised and late for everything, a dreamer with grandiose ideas, but a nicer chap you couldn't have met. I can't believe he's dead." He blew his cheeks out. "I mean, I really can't believe it. How on earth could an experienced boater like Graham fall overboard?"

"Was the, um, body wearing a lifejacket?" I asked.

"That's a valid question. I can ask. Graham would always have worn a lifejacket. He had an inflatable red one; I can picture him in it." He clenched his teeth and rocked his head. "Why? How?" He bit his lower lip. "Even if he'd fallen into the sea by mistake, Wednesday night was calm. He could've swum back to his boat and climbed aboard." He thumped the table. "There's something not right about all this."

I gave him a consoling look. He was going through the stages of grief, and now we were witnessing the denial bit.

The inappropriate sound of AC/DC heralded Oscar's phone again, and he rubbed his face to compose himself before answering it. "Hello? Yes, Oscar speaking. Good afternoon, Sergeant Will. Yes, I have heard; the mayor told me. Isn't it tragic?" He covered the mouthpiece and mouthed, 'The police'.

"Me?" continued Oscar. "I knew him well, yes, but surely you can find someone else? Someone closer to the deceased? What about Mrs Woodhatch?"

Emily and I glanced at each other, and we both shrugged.

"I see," continued Oscar's side of the phone call. "Quite understandable, poor woman." He looked at his watch. "It's 5:00 p.m. now. Will tomorrow morning be okay? Right. See you then. Goodbye, Sergeant." He pressed 'end' and stared at his phone.

We waited silently.

Oscar puffed upward, stared wide-eyed and shook his head slowly. "That was the sergeant. He wants me to identify the body."

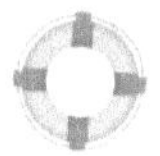

CHAPTER TEN

Anthony Blakey rubbed his hands together so hard, pieces of skin flaked from his fingers, and he washed them in the sink of his bed-and-breakfast accommodation. His surroundings were a step down from his usual London abode, but he would've slept in a shed if it meant he'd see her again. Maybe even touch her. He pressed his palms together in silent prayer.

The deed was done.

The man had been killed, and the body had been found on the beach.

His plan was exactly on track.

A stroll past the Marine Rescue station found the doors shuttered, and he tugged his hat lower to ensure the security cameras couldn't identify his face.

Shiraz wasn't there today. But, searching for coffee, Anthony Blakey had peered through the door of the café next door and seen her conversing with the councillor. The retired police officer whose face was on the council website. He'd almost burst in, accosted her and blown his entire operation. He had to restrain himself.

If he was going to know her, to touch her, to own her, he'd have to be patient.

Slow and steady wins the race.

That ex-police sergeant.

He was the key. He could introduce him to Shiraz.

In fact, the way Anthony envisioned his plan, Shiraz would be desperate to know him better.

CHAPTER ELEVEN

Saturday afternoon found me taking a bracing stroll around the harbour, the steaming, double shot, skinny latte I'd collected from the Wicked Whelk warming my hands. Although the wind was nothing like as strong as Thursday's gale, the stiff southerly breeze stirred up the sea, and waves slop-slop-slopped against the harbour wall, meaning I was the only participant enjoying this form of exercise today. Creaks and pings from the rigging of the fishing boats moored safely in Redcliff's harbour added a rhythmic soundtrack to my walk, and I grinned and tightened my favourite Burberry coat around my shoulders as I stepped out.

My strides were long, and I hummed as I marched. After almost twenty years being my husband's spare part, laughingly referred to as 'his better half', I was finally my own person. All my life, people had referred to me as 'Monty's wife', or 'Shiraz Jones, wife of Monty Jones'. Not 'Shiraz Jones, strong, single woman'. Not 'Shiraz Jones, marine rescue superhero'.

Definitely not 'Shiraz Jones, deceased deputy mayor investigator'. No way was I getting myself into another investigation. I had no stakes in this one at all.

The wind blew my hair into complicated knots, and I wondered how I'd ever untangle it. Thank goodness I wasn't carrying a pocket mirror. I didn't have any desire to see what might reflect from that.

Jim Turner's boat, the *Anstruther Pirate*, floated in its berth against the harbour wall. I wondered when I'd have the chance to listen to his pirate stories. The entire tale of Blakey's Island fascinated me, and I was determined to ask Murph if we could land there tomorrow. Not least because I wanted to find that rowing boat we'd seen. *Ruth*, it had said on the stern. I inspected the names of all the fishing fleet in the harbour, to see if any were called *Ruth* anything, and caught myself.

Am I looking for clues?

I shook my head and continued looking at the boats.

Some of their names were standard, boring, if you asked me. Members of the commercial fishing fleet, for instance.

The Redcliff Voyager. Seriously? Couldn't they think of anything more exciting?

The Amanda II. I presumed the owner was Amanda I. Or maybe Amanda was the owner's wife?

The Sea Shanty. Pff. How yawn-inducingly traditional.

Then there were the punny names. These boats were used for daytrippers, like Jim Turner's vessel.

Vitamin Sea. Cod Squad. Reel Estate. Seas the Day.

I liked them. They brought a smile to my lips.

And finally, the cryptic pleasure-boat names which challenged me to think.

Maid of Pleighwood. I worked that one out quickly.

She Kept the House. I wondered if the owner lived aboard this one.

And one simply called *The Office*. I had to think very hard about this. Until I realised 'The Office' must've been the owner's reply, when their partner asked where they were going.

But none called *Ruth*. That tender would remain a mystery.

I reached the end of the harbour wall and swivelled on my heels. The return journey was infinitely more pleasant, as the wind was now behind me. 1:30 p.m. Time to return to the café to help Emily clear up.

"Shiraz, not like that. What are you doing?" Emily stood beside me in the Wicked Whelk kitchen with a fierce look on her face as if I'd accidentally served her customers cat biscuits.

"Loading the dishwasher. Like you showed me."

"Small plates at the back, large plates at the front. Bowls on top."

"Does it matter?"

"Of course it matters. The way you're doing it, they won't clean properly, and then I'll have to wash them by hand."

My offer to be Emily's café assistant in return for accommodation upstairs was going from bad to worse. I wasn't sure I'd ever stacked a dishwasher before. Certainly not a commercial one. I mean, honestly, I'd been used to having staff at home in London. When would I have had the chance to practice?

"And where did you put my sharp knives?" asked Emily, opening every drawer in the hope the offending articles would magically spring out at her.

"The dirty ones? In the cutlery tray of the dishwasher."

"Noooo!" She tugged out the top shelf of the machine and rescued assorted-length black-handled utensils. "The Wusthof set don't go in there. They must be washed by hand. The dishwasher'll ruin them."

"What's the point of having a dishwasher if it can't clean things?" I muttered under my breath.

"Pardon?" said Emily, as she ran a sink full of hot water.

"Nothing." I returned to stacking the dishes and wondered whether I should start scanning the *Headland Bay Times* property rental pages for a new place to live. Then I paused. I loved the company. Emily was a good friend. Probably the most genuine friend I'd ever had. And if I was going to hang on to my accommodation arrangement, I'd better learn to stack the dishwasher the way she liked it. Even if it was ridiculously pedantic.

"Hi, Oscar."

I heard Emily call out, lifted my head from the plate drawer and banged it on an open cupboard.

"Are you all right, Shiraz?" said Oscar's voice, as I rubbed the back of my scalp, gritted my teeth and squeezed my eyes closed.

"Give me a minute to recover. This, um, catering lark requires skills I haven't yet learnt."

Emily laughed. "You're doing fine."

"Really?" My head throbbed, and I grimaced at her.

"Really. I appreciate the help. Sit down to recover, and I'll bring you both a drink."

"Thanks. Super-strong, skinny latte please. Triple shot."

"Triple shot?"

"Triple shot. The best medicine for a banged head."

"If you say so. Black Earl Grey tea, Oscar?"

"Please." He scraped a chair across the floor and sat at one of the tables.

I perched opposite him. "What's new? Have you been to identify Graham Woodhatch's body?"

"I have," said Oscar in a steady, low-pitched voice. "This case gets odder and odder."

"I love that you call it a case," said Emily as she placed cups in front of us. "This is all very Hercule Poirot."

"Why is it odd?" I asked. "It was Graham, right?"

Oscar shrugged. "It must be, I suppose. It had his unruly mop of black hair which he never cut properly. It was his height and the right stocky build.

"But...?

"But his face was so smashed in I couldn't positively identify him." Oscar sighed.

"So what happened?"

"I asked if they had anything else to help me. And they showed me his phone, which didn't work anymore, and his wallet, which they found in his pocket. It contained a soggy photo of his wife, other ruined bits of paper, receipts and such like, a driving licence, bank cards and loyalty cards, all with the name Graham Woodhatch on them. So I told Sergeant Will, even though the poor chap's face was too badly damaged to positively identify him, I considered there was enough with the wallet contents, the hair and the body shape to say it was Graham."

He ran his hand back through his hair. "As we discussed yesterday, it couldn't be anyone else, could it? No one reported any other missing boaters. But I still can't believe Graham drowned. The police have released the boat, and it's tied up on its usual mooring. I don't know what his wife will do with it. She worked in his shop occasionally, but she's not interested in boating."

Emily turned to me. "Sorry to change the subject but, Shiraz, have you revised your lateral and cardinal mark day shapes for Sunday's training? Murph's testing us, remember?"

"Are you out on the rescue boat this weekend?" asked Oscar.

I nodded. "Yep. Murph wants to educate us on local hazards. We've seen the warning lights around Blakey's Island; now he wants to show us the same markers during the day."

"Ah. I may spot you out there. That hotel director chap, Johnny Chadwick, has invited the mayor and the councillors for drinks and nibbles on the company yacht. We'll be circling Blakey's Island and viewing the location of the proposed development. The other directors will be on board too. Complete bribery, but they're defending it on the grounds the entire council's invited, not just the 'no' voters."

"Drinks and nibbles?" asked Emily. "They didn't ask me to provide catering for a yacht."

"I told you; these guys will have their own chefs and food supplies. I honestly don't think the Wicked Whelk will benefit from this construction activity at all. But don't let me try to influence you. If this ever goes to public ballot, your vote might make the difference."

"There are no company yachts in the harbour," I said. "I walked around there this morning and saw the usual fishing vessels and private boats. I'm imagining this yacht'll be vast, something like my husband's PR firm used to own."

My mind dwelt on a sudden flashback to a time spent feeling like a piece of meat, standing on the bow of Monty's white gin palace, waving to photographers as we left port, with film stars or even royalty on board.

"I understand the yacht lives in Brighthaven," continued Oscar, "the next town around the coast past Headland Bay. The skipper and crew are bringing her to Redcliff, and they'll moor her against the harbour wall tomorrow morning."

"I can't wait to see that," said Emily. "I've never seen one of those flash cruisers except on *Hawaii Five-0*."

"It might surprise you to learn I haven't either," said Oscar. "I'll give you a report and show you photos, if I'm allowed to take them."

"We'll wave as we pass," said Emily. "Perhaps you could throw us a canape?"

"I'm sure whatever fare we're served won't be up to your standard. Here, let me pay for the drinks."

"Nonsense, Oscar. I can't charge my friends for coffee."

"No, I insist. I've enjoyed so many hot drinks at your expense." He pulled out his wallet, frowned and turned it over. "That's odd. This isn't mine."

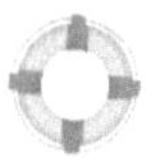

CHAPTER TWELVE

Oscar slapped his forehead. "Silly me. I must've left my wallet at the police station and picked up Graham Woodhatch's by mistake."

I pointed at the battered, discoloured brown article in Oscar's hand. "You're sure that's Graham's?"

"Yes. See?" He unbuttoned the wallet and pulled out a driving licence and several other cards. "That photo's very out of date. Graham was in his fifties; he looks around thirty in the picture."

I spread out the cards on the table between us and inspected them. "It's not only the photo. Everything's out of date. The driving licence expired several years ago. The credit cards both lapsed last year, and the loyalty cards have also all run out."

"Graham wasn't the most organised man." Oscar picked up the cards and stuffed them back into the wallet. "It doesn't surprise me he hadn't got around to renewing his licence or bank cards." He stood. "I'll head back to the police station and retrieve my wallet. Sorry, Emily. I'll have to pay you next time."

"Really, it doesn't matter. What's a hot drink between friends?"

Dinner in Emily's flat was about to comprise café leftovers. In fact, all we ever ate were café leftovers or take away fish and chips. I'm certain if the Wicked Whelk had served fish and chips we could've combined the two experiences. On the plus side, I never had to pay for a meal, but honestly, I would've preferred to eat out now and then. Maybe you can take the girl out of the city, but not take the city out of the girl?

Goodness, I hope not.

"What's our meal tonight, Emily?"

"Chicken pies. I make everything without additives and preservatives, so they won't keep until tomorrow."

"Um, your chicken pies are delicious. I don't suppose you have any lettucy-type things to go with them? My stomach's crying out for greens."

"Sorry. I threw out all the leftover salad from the filled rolls yesterday. There's bread? If it's stale, we could toast it?"

"I'll tell you what, Emily. Why don't I treat us both to a meal at one of Redcliff's eateries?"

"Really? Um, that'd be lovely. But I can't stay out too late. The café won't open itself at 6:00 a.m."

"Is there anywhere you'd recommend? I don't mean a silver-service, five-course banquet; something simple."

"There's the Smuggler's Tavern. They do good food. Gosh, I haven't been out to dinner for ages, on account of, um, not having anyone to go with."

"I thought you preferred your own company? Introvert and all that. A glass of Sauvignon Blanc and a book."

"I do. But now and then, it'd be nice to have someone to split a bottle of wine with. That's to say, apart from you. You know what I mean."

I laughed. "Okay, tonight we'll go out to the pub for dinner. We'll share a bottle of wine, and…"

Emily held up her hand. "I'm only having one glass. And I'll be in bed by nine as usual. You're not going to lead me astray into all your London debauchery and nightclubbing. The only cavorting I ever do is at the Marine Rescue Christmas Barn Dance."

"Don't worry; I'll drink most of it as I don't have to be up as early as you, and we'll have a chat. A good girl-to-girl chat about girly things."

"You're on. I enjoy having you to stay, Shiraz. You're good company without being too demanding."

"What's that supposed to imply?"

"I mean, you don't have an agenda. Apart from marine rescue training. I'll pull on shoes, and we'll head out."

"You're going like that?"

She glanced down at her track pants and hoody top. "Yes. Why not?"

"Um, no reason. Wait for me. I won't be a minute."

I dashed into my bedroom, disturbing Boots, who slept on my bed, and wondered how I was going to do my makeup, straighten my hair and choose a stunning outfit in the time it took Emily to put on her shoes. We may've been only going to the pub, but a girl's got to make an impression, right? When I'd walked into a London restaurant, all the diners' heads swivelled and at least one flashbulb popped.

Okay, the white roll-neck Tom Ford jumper. Warm enough for a winter's night, fashionable enough to show my figure. My Ghost, slim-fit black jeans. This could be a challenge; they often took five minutes of wiggling whilst lying on my back just to do up the zip. And my Stuart Weitzman brown, heeled, thigh-length boots. I was five foot ten before I put them on, six feet tall after. Poor Emily, I'd be looking down at her again. Not metaphorically, I mean; literally. I'd really have to encourage her to wear some decent heels soon. I tugged the jumper over my head and was just beginning the horizontal fight with the jeans, when Emily walked in.

She frowned at me and tilted her head. "Why are you lying down?"

"I'm trying to pull these jeans on."

"Watch out. Be careful not to squash Boots. What was wrong with what you were wearing?"

"I can't go to an eating establishment in joggers."

"It's the Smuggler's Tavern. People drink there straight from the fishing boats. Come on."

"So?" I inched the jeans to my hips, jumped to my feet and bounced a few times to pull them up the last few inches. This action alarmed Boots, who jumped off my bed and hid in the corner. "If you want me to be quicker, could you switch on the hair straighteners?"

"These things?"

"The tongs that say 'GHD' on them. Push the button on top until they beep."

"What does GHD stand for?"

"Good Hair Day. They're the best straighteners. I've tried so many other brands: Vidal Sassoon, Paul Mitchell, T3, and I can't find anything to beat them."

Emily picked them up and turned them on. I heard the reassuring diddle-dee sound of them coming to life as she turned them over in her hand.

"Careful," I said. "They get super-hot."

"What do they do?"

"What it says on the tin. Straighten your hair."

"But you have such beautiful waves. I wish I had hair like yours. Mine's boring."

I laughed. "We always want what we don't have. I always wished my hair was straight like yours. So easy to manage." I ran tresses of hair through the blades of the straighteners, which sizzled as they worked. "See? This is how I get ready for a night out."

"Hmm. It sounds like you're frying your fringe. Are you ready now?"

"I'll put on some makeup; then we'll go. Which earrings d'you like?"

I opened my jewellery box, and Emily's eyes opened as wide as coffee cups. She sucked in a breath. "Shiraz, these are so beautiful. Are those real diamonds?"

"Of course they are."

"And sapphires? Is that an emerald?"

"All the genuine articles. Would you like to borrow a pair?"

She blushed. "Me? In diamonds?"

"Why not? But they won't go with that hoodie and slacks. We'll have to find something else. D'you have any smart jeans? I would lend you a pair, but mine would be too long."

"I have some white ones I've never worn. I found them in a charity shop."

"Fetch them. And we'll see if we can find you a top." Emily nipped to her room, and I rummaged through my wardrobe. What would go with white jeans? White top? No, she'd look like a polar bear. Grey top? Drab. How about my biscuit-coloured Gucci jumper? That'd make a statement.

Emily returned wearing the trousers, looking uncomfortable. "These are the jeans. But I look silly in them."

"They're made by G-Star Raw. Pretty good for a charity shop purchase. They're very fashionable. And they suit you."

"No, they don't. Don't be silly. I'll take them off."

"Try this top on with them. And these heels. I know the shoes will be too big for you, but stand in front of the mirror for me with them on. Please?"

"Okay, but I'm taking them off again straight away." Emily tugged the Gucci jumper over her head and slipped on my brown wedges.

I stood behind her as she looked in the mirror. "And now, the finishing touch. I held my Tiffany & Co. diamond earrings up to her lobes and peered over her shoulder. "Cinder-Emily, you shall go to the ball."

Emily bit her lip, and a tear ran down one cheek.

I laid the earrings down and clutched her shoulders. "What's wrong? Why are you crying?"

"You're my best friend, Shiraz. I've never known anyone like you. You believe in me. Silly little Emily, the café girl." She wiped her eyes and slipped off one heel. "I'll take these clothes off now."

"No!" I stamped my foot. "Keep them on. For me. For tonight. Please? You look so good. Can you walk in those shoes?"

Emily did a test step and grabbed my arm. "I think so. If you're next to me." She gave me a watery smile. "Catch me if I fall."

"That's my girl. Put on the earrings while I finish in the bathroom. Then we'll head out for a night on the town."

"Gosh." She clenched her teeth and raised her eyebrows. "I hope I don't see too many people I know."

I ducked my head to enter the door of the Smuggler's Tavern and stepped down into the public bar. Emily hid behind me and gripped my coat to steady herself. My wedges were at least one size too big for her, and the stroll along the seafront had incorporated some interesting dance moves. I had to remember she wasn't accustomed to people admiring her looks and dress sense.

We approached the bar, which was propped up by an assortment of ruddy-faced fishermen and women dressed in outdoor wear.

"Hi," I asked. "Are you serving food?"

The barman did a double take as he looked up. His gaze then swung to Emily, and he gave her a puzzled look of partial recognition. I expected him to say, 'We don't see your type around here too often,' but he said nothing as his mouth opened and closed silently. He plucked two menus from a stack behind him, lifted a hatch in the bar and indicated we should follow him. All eyes were on us as we crossed the floor. I could've sworn a quiet wolf whistle came from one of the dark corners. My head was held high, but Emily tried to make herself even smaller than she was. The barman seated us at a table for two, stared at us again, then returned to his duties.

"I almost fell over in the heels again," whispered Emily. "Let's eat quick-smart, then get out of here. I know some of these people."

"Take off your coat." I grinned at her. "We're not going anywhere yet. What's your favourite Champagne?"

"Champagne? Do they serve Champagne in the Smuggler's Tavern? I don't think I've drunk it except at weddings and christenings."

"The menu says they have Bollinger and Lanson. I prefer Bolly. Lanson's a little sweet."

"If you say so. Remember, I'm only having one glass." She hung her coat on the back of her chair and glanced left and right. The fishing population returned to their conversations about haddock and nets, or whatever they discussed, and they lost interest in us.

Except for one chap.

One chap we both knew well.

97

CHAPTER THIRTEEN

David from Marine Rescue approached our table and crouched beside us.

"Shiraz? You look so different out of uniform. And Emily, I barely recognise you. What's the occasion?"

"Hi, David," said Emily. She picked her nails and studied her lap.

"No special occasion," I said to him. "Us girls like to dress up sometimes for the sake of it."

"Could I buy you a drink, Emily?" he asked. He couldn't take his eyes off her.

Maybe they're suited? He's definitely too young for me.

Emily blushed like an over-ripe strawberry. "It's okay, David. Shiraz was ordering Champagne. We're having dinner together."

"Oh. When you finish eating, come over and say 'Hi'. I'm with my friends at the end of the bar."

"We'll see," I said. "Emily wants to get to bed early. She has to open the café at six in the morning."

"That'd be lovely," said Emily, completely ignoring me. "It'd be great to get to know you outside of Marine Rescue."

"See you soon, then." David's eyes met Emily's, then he turned away and sauntered back to the bar.

"D'you think he likes me?" she asked. "I've always thought he was far too good for someone like me. At training, he knows everything." She glanced over toward his group.

"Too good for you? Emily Philpot, maybe *you're* too good for *him*? Ever thought of that? Ah, here's the waitress. Could we have a bottle of Bollinger please?"

"Bollinger?"

"Yes. Champagne." I showed her the line on the menu. "And I'll have the steak. Rare to Medium, please. With chips and salad. Emily, have you decided?"

"The chicken pie, please."

"Wasn't that what we were having at home?"

"I'm sure this one'll be fresher. And it comes with vegetables." She glanced around and fiddled with her cutlery.

The Bollinger arrived in a metal ice bucket with two flutes. Condensation dripped down the side of the bottle as the server eased the cork out and poured two glasses. "Cheers, Emily," I said. "Let's drink to..."

"Love," said Emily. "We'll drink to love, and Emily not being single anymore."

"Um, okay. To love," I echoed. We clinked glasses.

"How was the chicken pie?" I asked, as Emily laid her knife and fork together.

"Mmm. I think the ones I make are better. Is there any Champagne left?"

"It goes down easily, doesn't it? Sorry, we finished the bottle."

"The entire bottle? You must have drunk almost all of it. I only had one glass."

"One glass three times." I grinned. "For someone who hasn't drunk Bollinger before, you certainly enjoyed it."

"Gosh." Emily sucked in a breath. "I hope I don't gain a taste for it. The café doesn't provide me with funds for a Champagne lifestyle."

I leant my chin in my hands and stared at her. "This has been such a lovely evening, Emily. We must do it more often. I'm so pleased you liked the Champagne."

"This won't be a habit, Shiraz. I still feel silly in all this finery. Now, if you'll excuse me, I must visit the little girls' room." She pushed herself up and wobbled towards the rear of the tavern.

A quick glance at her feet revealed she was barefoot, and I checked the underside of the table to ensure my wedges were still there. It was probably best she didn't wear them after three glasses of Bolly; remaining vertical might be a challenge. I reached into my handbag and was unlocking my phone when a familiar man wearing a trench coat and trilby hat materialised beside the table.

"Shiraz," he said. "What a coincidence." He noticed the empty plate opposite me. "Sorry, am I intruding on a date?"

"Hello, Oscar. I should be so lucky. Emily and I were having a girls' night out. She's just popped to the ladies'. Do you come in here often? I didn't know you were a pub goer."

"Not regularly, but"—he bent his head to my level—"I received a strange phone call today." He placed a pint of beer on the table. For some reason, he wore a red carnation in his buttonhole, and I wondered if he'd been to a wedding.

I indicated Emily's empty chair. "Take a seat. Tell me about it."

"Okay, just briefly. I'm supposed to be meeting a man, but I don't know what he looks like."

"You are being mysterious. Spill the beans."

I tipped the dregs of my Champagne back and considered ordering a second bottle, then remembered Emily had to be up early and put the thought to one side.

"This phone call I received," said Oscar. "It came this afternoon, after I returned from seeing you at the café. The caller seemed to know who I was and my role on the council. He intimated he had crucial information which could block the hotel development for good. Of course, that pricked my ears up, and I asked him to continue."

"You're sure he wasn't some crank?"

"I was a police officer for over thirty years, and I like to think I have an ear for these things. He wouldn't be led on details, but he stated he was connected with Blakey's Island. I couldn't understand what this meant. The island's public land owned by the council; I wondered if he'd worked there as a warden before Graham Woodhatch, but he didn't sound old enough. He didn't want to go into details over the phone, and he asked if I'd meet him."

"Gosh. This is all very secret squirrel, isn't it?"

"Indeed. He wanted to rendezvous at eight this evening, down at the harbour. I refused. The harbour's deserted at night; there are only one or two streetlights, and there would've been no one around. I had no idea what this man wanted, but I wasn't going to meet someone I'd never spoken to before in a deserted location. That'd be asking for trouble."

"Quite. Although it doesn't sound like he was about to mug you and steal your wallet."

"No. Oh, and talking about wallets, I've retrieved mine from the police station. Constable Bert was rather embarrassed he'd allowed me to walk off with the deceased's possessions."

"I'll bet he was. But back to your mysterious caller?"

"I told him in no uncertain terms I'd be happy to meet him, but in a public place. I suggested here, at the Smuggler's Tavern. Reluctantly, he agreed, and we arranged that I'd have a flower pinned to my lapel so he could identify me. I also asked his name, but he would only reveal he was called Anthony."

"Very John Le Carré. So where is he?"

"Turn around slowly and look over your right shoulder. I think this might be him now."

A man stood in the doorway, and a gust of cold air accompanied his entrance. My first impression was of his immaculate dress sense. He wore a sharp, charcoal suit, a long, midnight-black overcoat and a crisp white shirt with a thin, dark tie. Light from the pub's fire reflected in his gold cufflinks. He'd attracted the attention of the regular clientèle, who'd not only had to put up with Emily and me arriving as if we were about to attend a film premiere, but now had this dark stranger in their midst. I expected the music to stop playing until someone spoke, but this wasn't a cowboy movie, and it didn't.

The new arrival glanced around, and his gaze settled on Oscar, who stood and nodded. The man marched confidently towards us, ignoring everyone else.

Oscar held out his hand. "Anthony?"

The man spoke with a deep, private-school-educated voice. "Yes." He glanced at the flower. "You must be Oscar Wainwright. And who is your delightful companion?"

Oscar held one palm towards me. "This is my, um, associate, Shiraz Jones."

The man looked familiar, but out of place. Like when you coincidentally bump into your next-door-neighbour at a foreign airport. I stood and held out my hand.

He bowed and kissed it, in a very un-PC gesture which left me with a mingling tingle of discomfort and excitement.

"Ms Jones. Anthony Blakey, at your service."

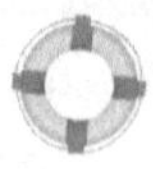

CHAPTER FOURTEEN

I gasped. Oscar's eyes widened.

"Blakey?" I said. "As in...?"

"As in the pirate, Ms Jones. As in the pirate. May I?" He dragged a chair from a neighbouring table and gestured we should all sit. I hadn't seen a man who took such care with his dress since my days on the red carpet, and I felt like I should find him attractive. His deep, cultured voice reassured me, but there was something about him I couldn't put my finger on, and I subconsciously leant away. His gaze wavered from me to Oscar, and it wasn't clear who was supposed to speak next.

So I did. "You don't look like a pirate, Mr, um, Blakey."

"Have you ever met a pirate?"

"Well, no, but..."

"Maybe, Ms Jones, they all look like me?"

He swept his hands down his front, indicating his suit, and my mouth opened but no words came out.

I should find you attractive, but there's something not…

Oscar cleared his throat. "You wanted to meet with me in confidence."

"Indeed, I did. Is there somewhere quieter we could go? As your associate, Ms Jones is welcome to accompany us."

"Will this take long?" I asked. "I'm here with a friend."

"For our initial meeting, no," said Anthony. "But I suspect, once you've heard my plan, our subsequent rendezvous may be lengthier."

Rendezvous. A shiver ran up and down my spine.

"How about the family bar?" asked Oscar. "No one with young children will be dining at this time in the evening."

"Very well," said Anthony. "It's important we're not overheard."

We stood, and I glanced around to see where Emily had got to. I found the back of her blonde bob among David's group, and I heard her laugh.

Emily's getting on well with the boys. Good for her. I wonder what being a pirate's girl would be like.

Oscar opened the door to the pub's family area, which, as he predicted, was empty. Tables were laid for a future meal, toys in the corner had been tidied neatly and the lights behind the servery betrayed the absence of staff. We sat at a table for four.

Oscar tapped his fingers together. "So, Anthony Blakey, if indeed that is your name, what d'you have to tell us?"

The dark stranger held up one finger. "Mr Wainwright, I understand your skepticism of my name, but once you've heard my story, I think you and I will be best friends. And so will we, Ms Jones." He laid his hand on top of mine, and I tugged it back slightly. My emotions tore between lust and revulsion, both powerful feelings.

Oscar leant back and folded his arms.

"First," said Anthony. "May I express my condolences at your colleague's passing? I..."

Oscar frowned and leant forward. "How on earth did you know about that?"

"I'm a well-connected man, with a keen interest in Redcliff events."

"Your dress indicates prosperity and success. Why would you be concerned with little old Redcliff?"

Anthony lowered his voice and pointed at his chest. "I, Anthony Blakey, am a direct descendant of the infamous pirate Thomas Blakey, who terrorised these shores over two hundred years ago."

"Prove it," said Oscar, leaning back, folding his arms and narrowing his eyes.

The dark stranger pursed his lips and nodded slowly. His immaculately manicured hand reached into an inner pocket of his coat and extracted a leather wallet. He plucked a business card from it, laid it on the table and slid it towards us.

I picked it up, then showed it to Oscar, who turned it over and back again in his hand. "Anyone can have a business card printed saying anything."

Anthony Blakey leant forward and met Oscar's stare, as if they were opponents in a game of chess. "It disappoints me you doubt my credentials, when I'm here to lend weight to your cause. Very well. Since you insist, will this persuade you?" He removed another card from his wallet and slid it over the table. "My driving licence."

Oscar lifted the credit-card sized document and inspected it. "This says your name's Anthony Blakey. It does *not* prove you're descended from the pirate."

"Humour me. Let's say I am. Let's say I have evidence. What would that mean for your campaign to prevent the hotel being built?"

"How d'you know about that?"

"You'd be surprised who reads Redcliff Council minutes."

"You're probably the only person who does."

"What would it mean to the 'no' campaign, Mr Wainwright, if a descendant of Thomas Blakey, the pirate, turned up in Redcliff and lay claim to Blakey's Island?"

"It'd put the cat amongst the pigeons," said Oscar. "The entire proposal's based on the premise that Redcliff Council has the right to lease the island to Chadwick-Mappin International Hotels. If the island belongs to someone else, they no longer have that right. Which means…"

I felt it was time for me to contribute. "Mr Chadwick and his colleagues would have to negotiate with you, Mr Blakey, instead of the council."

"Actually, Ms Jones," said Anthony, "they'd need to negotiate with both me and the council. Me to lease the land, and the council to permit the development. But obviously, they can't permit a hotel to be built if I don't agree."

"How would we prove you owned the island?" asked Oscar.

Anthony slitted his eyes, leant forward and grabbed Oscar's forearm. "I appreciate your use of the word 'we'. Because this operation is going to require teamwork."

Oscar shook his head. "I haven't committed to anything. But if what you say is true, this is an industrial-sized spanner in the works for the mayor and her little scheme. Go on, how would you show you had a legitimate claim to the island?"

"Let's say I have a document. A lease of the island to Thomas Blakey the pirate and his descendants in perpetuity."

"Can we see this document?" I asked, not least because I wanted to hear his voice speak to me again.

"All in good time, Ms Jones. At our next meeting, perhaps. In the meantime, I..."

CRASH

The door from the public bar burst open, and Emily landed with a WHUMP on the floor.

CHAPTER FIFTEEN

"Gosh, Emily. Are you okay?" I rushed to help, as David appeared in the doorway behind.

"I warned her," he said, "but she wouldn't listen."

Emily pushed herself to her knees and fell again. I tugged her up by lifting under her armpits.

"Give me a hand. She's like a limp rag doll. What did you warn her about, David? What have you done to her?"

"Hey, I haven't done anything. She came over to ask what we were drinking, so we offered her a glass."

"Oh, no. She'd already demolished half a bottle of Bollinger. This is all my fault. She's not used to being a party girl. Um, what did you give her?"

Emily's face whitened and sweat ran down her cheeks. She tried to speak, but her words were so indistinct, I gave up at the first 'blah-rah-rah-blaaah'.

"We had jugs of the local cider," said David. "From Merton's farm. Potent stuff. I told her it was stronger than it tasted."

"Especially if you're not used to it. How much did she have?"

"Maybe a pint? I'm not sure. We topped her up at least once."

"So, possibly two pints? Great. David, you and I are going to take her home. You lift her under one arm, and I'll take the other."

"Can you guys manage without me?" asked Oscar. "I'll say goodbye to Anthony." He turned around. "That's strange. Where did he go?"

"Never mind about him. This is an emergency. Oscar, I'll need you to hold the doors. David: one, two, three, lift."

We carried Emily out of the side entrance and began the slow stagger along the seafront. Thankfully, on this frosty night, there were no late pedestrians to witness her progression. With every three steps forward being augmented by two sideways and one backward, we took an eternity to reach the Wicked Whelk.

"Are we—hic—going to another party?" asked Emily's mouth, which had possibly become disconnected from her brain.

"No, we are not going to any more parties. We're taking you home, and you're drinking a pint of water and going to bed. I don't know how you'll open the café tomorrow, but we'll deal with that when we get to it."

"I'll be fine," slurred Emily. "I'll be absholly fine."

This wasn't the first time I'd helped a drunken companion home by a long way, but my so-called friends in London had lived this existence every weekend. They certainly didn't have any responsibilities beyond ensuring photos of them passed out in a stranger's front garden didn't enter the society pages. Unless they wanted them to, and the paparazzi could be persuaded to attend at the appropriate moment.

None of them owned cafés.

We reached our front door, and I leant Emily against it while I fumbled in her bag for the key. I gave it to Oscar to unlock.

"D'you need my help still?" asked David. "My friends'll wonder where I am."

"Hey, you're not going anywhere, Mister." I jabbed a finger at him. "You got her into this mess."

"I didn't get her drunk," spluttered David. "You said she'd had half a bottle of Champagne before she drank anything with me."

"Whatever. I need your help to take her upstairs."

The door opened, and I grabbed Emily before she fell through it.

"We can't carry her up the steps; they're too narrow and steep. Oscar, thanks; we'll take it from here. David, you push her from behind and make sure she doesn't fall backwards; I'll take her arms and tug her up. Ready?"

Our strange procession ascended the stairs one step at a time. I honestly believed Emily had little cognisance of what was going on, and I began to feel sorry for her. I'd been in this state many times myself, and I knew the last thing any drunk person needed was their friends berating them.

Once we reached the top of the stairs, we carried her to her bedroom and dumped her on the bed. Boots had taken up residence between her pillows and objected to his provider collapsing in front of him.

"Should I help you undress her?" asked David.

"Definitely not. That's a job for me alone. Fetch her a glass of water." I removed Emily's coat and jumper, then lay her back and tugged off her jeans. By the time David returned, she was under the duvet.

"See yourself out," I said. "I'll look after her from here. She needs to sleep it off."

David avoided my eyes. His steps echoed on the stairs, then the door to the street slammed.

Now what do I do? What if she's too ill to open the Wicked Whelk in the morning?

I glanced at Emily. The duvet rose and fell. At least she was breathing, but she'd have the granddaddy of all hangovers tomorrow. I prepared myself for bed and realised my wedges which Emily had borrowed were still at the pub. Hopefully, I could retrieve them tomorrow.

A series of crashes woke me.

Clock.

6:00 a.m.

What's going on?

I remembered.

The pub. The Bollinger. Emily drinking cider with David. Carrying her home.

I'm not a morning person at the best of times, so I turned over and hoped the crashing would stop.

It didn't.

The tinkle of shattering glass convinced me I should drag myself out of bed and investigate. I threw on clothes, walked into the kitchen and found Emily drinking from the tap.

"What are you doing? Have we run out of glasses?"

Emily raised her eyes, and I was met with a sight as if somebody had grabbed Medusa's head, dragged it through a gorse bush, then flushed it down the lavatory. "Shiraz, I am never touching alcohol again. Never. You and your Champagne. You're a bad influence."

"Was it the Champagne? Or was it the two pints of local cider?"

"I didn't drink any cider. Did I?"

"D'you remember anything about coming home? I carried you and put you to bed."

"Did you?"

"Yes. Me and David."

She covered her eyes. "Oh, no. Did David see me drunk?"

"David's the reason you were drunk. How d'you feel now?"

"Sick. Sick as anything. My mouth's as dry as stale toast. And I'm late opening the café. I have to go downstairs. But I can't." She ducked her head under the tap again and let it overflow between her lips.

I knew I was going to regret my next sentence. "I'll open the café. You're in no fit state to greet customers."

"How? You don't know how to chop a cucumber or load a dishwasher. What will you do about coffee? D'you even understand how to turn the machine on?"

"Hey, I'm trying to help here. What choice do we have? I'll work it out. Where's the café key?"

"On the hook behind the door. Tell the customers I'm coming. There's food in the fridge you can offer them. Can you make a toasted sandwich?"

"How hard can it be? Two bits of bread with something between them. I'll manage." I swiped the key, shoved a cap on my head to disguise my bed-hair and clumped down the stairs.

"Shiraz," called Emily as I opened the door to the street. "Thank you. I'll be there as soon as I feel human again."

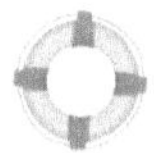

Three customers queued outside the café door, dressed in clothes that identified them as some of Emily's commercial fishing regulars.

"Morning," said one. "No Emily today?"

"Um, she's not very well. I'll be happy to serve you until she appears." I swung the door open, switched the light on and turned up the heater.

Good start. I strode behind the counter and faced the men as if I knew what I was doing.

Which I didn't.

"One tea, one latte and one cappuccino, please," said the man who'd spoken previously.

"Certainly." I jotted the order down confidently. "Anything to eat?"

"Yes, please. The usual. Three bacon-and-egg toasted sandwiches."

"No problem. Won't be long."

I glanced left and right at the challenge I'd set myself. Why did the catering equipment look so complicated from this side of the counter? What was that switch with 'Do Not Turn Off' stuck to it? Where would I find eggs? Thank goodness there weren't more customers at this early hour. Now would not be too soon for Emily to make an appearance, no matter what state she was in.

I clicked a switch on the wall and lit up a reassuring glow from the front of the coffee machine. Regardless of how long the customers had to wait, my first, vital task would be to make myself a double shot, skinny latte.

How does Emily do this? Scoop coffee beans out of somewhere, grind them, tap them into the holder thing, then twist it, and coffee comes out of the bottom. Easy.

I discovered the coffee beans, emptied some into the hopper at the top of the machine and heard the wonderful, crunchy sound of them grinding. Next, I clicked the machine as I'd seen Emily do, and released the coffee grounds into the little container. The rich, roasted smell of caffeine heaven permeated through the air, and I smiled and gave myself a thumbs-up. I tamped the coffee down, clipped in the holder and realised I had no idea what the difference was between making a latte and making a cappuccino. Hopefully, no one could tell. Let's move onto the toasted sandwiches.

Three bacon and egg. Easy. I opened the toasting machine and discovered to my joy there was enough space to cook four sandwiches at once, so I placed rashers of bacon on top of four slices of wholemeal bread.

Looking good.

I glanced over at the three customers, but thankfully they weren't looking my way. Then I cracked an egg on top of the first rasher, which immediately ran everywhere and spilt out of the sides of the machine and onto the worktop.

Nooo. How can one little egg contain so much liquid?

The coffee machine began to steam and burble behind me, and a shot of black liquid squirted into the drip tray, which overflowed onto the floor.

Disaster. Help!

I was on my knees, in the process of using an entire roll of kitchen towel to mop up black coffee and raw egg mixed together, when I heard a female voice above me.

"D'you need help, love? You certainly look like you do."

I pushed myself up and met eyes with a rosy-cheeked, middle-aged woman with shoulder-length, dark, curly hair.

"Is everything okay?" She frowned at me. "What happened here?"

I must've looked a state. Egg and coffee covered my hands, and clumps of paper towel stuck to me. The egg white continued to drip out of the toastie machine, and the coffee maker emitted puffs of steam as if it were an enthusiastic train in a children's cartoon.

"Everything is not okay. I don't usually serve here."

"I can tell that," said the lady. She laughed.

"My friend runs this place," I continued, wiping my hands on a tea towel, "but she's not well. I have three coffees and three bacon-and-egg toasted sandwiches to make, and I've never made either in my life. If you know how to, you may be my new best friend."

She rolled her eyes and shook her head. "I do know that before you make a bacon-and-egg toasted sandwich, you cook the bacon and fry the egg. Here's what we'll do. You carry on clearing up your mess, and I'll make the toasted sandwiches. We'll work out the coffee machine between us. It can't be that hard. Goodness, I only popped in for a hot chocolate on my morning walk, and now I seem to be running the place."

She removed my attempts from the toasting machine and binned them, opened all the cupboards and found a frying pan. The welcome smell of cooked breakfast reached my nostrils. Thank goodness my father had never taken his religion seriously; I had no idea how I'd cope without bacon. I had zero idea who this person flipping eggs at the stove was, but she was all that stood between me and complete catastrophe. Thankfully, Emily owned two more rolls of kitchen towel, and I was about to finish both of them.

"Are you done down there?" asked the woman. "You keep an eye on these sandwiches, and I'll investigate this coffee machine."

She'd already cooked the bacon and eggs, placed fresh bread in the sandwich toaster and closed the lid. Sizzling announced the food's progression, and I opened the toastie machine to take a precautionary peek. I'd no idea how long my guardian angel would stay behind the counter, and the last thing I needed was to have to make a third round of sandwiches if these ones burnt.

The hot drink machine made noises which indicated coffee was about to be delivered in mugs and not over the linoleum.

"What coffees was it, love?"

I grabbed the pad I'd scribbled on so efficiently. "One latte, one cappuccino and one tea. Oh, and a double shot skinny latte for me. And whatever you want for yourself."

"Right-o. You take the sandwiches out of the toaster, plate them up and deliver them to your customers. I'll finish the drinks."

I glanced at my saviour and gave her a half smile as I opened the lid and removed the customers' breakfasts. "Thank you so much. I'm hopeless with cooking. Sorry, I didn't have a chance to introduce myself. I'm Shiraz Jones."

"I'm Angela," she said.

I carried the plates to the waiting customers. Angela followed me with the drinks.

"Thanks, Angela," I said, as we returned to the counter. "You're a lifesaver. Like me, I suppose. I volunteer with Marine Rescue next door."

"You're with Marine Rescue? I called you out on Wednesday night."

"Really? My hand flew to my mouth. "Oh! You're Graham Woodhatch's, um, widow?"

"I am, but that's not a title I'm at all accustomed to."

The tops of my cheeks tingled. "Of course you're not. I'm so sorry for your loss. Here, leave this all to me. I can manage."

"No, you can't."

"You're right, I can't. But I mustn't ask you to help, after all you've been through."

"Nonsense. I need something to occupy me. My friend told me I couldn't sit in the house moping all day, and I had to take my mind off things. And helping you out of your predicament does exactly that."

"My predicament's nothing compared to yours, Angela. What a terrible, terrible accident."

"Accident? That was no accident. There's no way my Graham would've fallen overboard. No indeed. He was murdered."

CHAPTER SIXTEEN

"Murdered?" I asked. Angela was clearly going through the stage of grief which blamed anyone or anything. "Who would've wanted to murder him?"

"Isn't it obvious?" she asked. "It was them."

"Who's them?"

"The hotel people. They approached Graham at the harbour when he was working on his boat and engaged him in conversation. Naturally, he thought they were friendly tourists. The chat moved onto fishing, Graham's first love. Then Graham mentioned he owned the fishing tackle shop in the High Street."

I was glad other customers didn't disturb our conversation. "So what does that have to do with the hotel development?"

"Those wretched people told Graham who they represented. And they cornered him against the harbour wall and said if he didn't vote to allow the development to go ahead, he could kiss his fishing shop business goodbye. That shop was his passion. Imagine your work involves doing something you love. It wouldn't be work, would it? His employment was his hobby, his lifestyle. He'd already lost one dream job as Blakey's Island warden, spending his days with the puffins, fishing off the island. Now these people were threatening him with losing another."

She covered her hand with her mouth, sobbed twice, and I gave her a look of commiseration.

"Sorry," she said. "Every time I think of him, every time I smell his pipe smoke on his clothes, I burst into tears."

I turned away from her and clenched my teeth. I needed to hear the rest of her story without looking like I was prying too much. And without any more customers coming in.

"Um, what was Graham's response?"

"Response, dear?"

"Yes, his response to the threat against his shop."

She took a deep breath. "He asked them how they intended to carry out their blackmail. Their answer made his blood run cold. Recently, ownership of his premises had changed hands. Graham hadn't taken any notice of this. He paid his rent to the same estate agent each month, so nothing altered for him."

"Are you saying the hotel developers bought his shop just to push their hotel plans through? They threatened him with eviction? That seems very extreme."

"That's exactly what they did. And when Graham spoke to other council members, he discovered one or two of them had received similar intimidation."

"Gosh. But the vote was split almost evenly. Obviously, they hadn't strong-armed enough councillors."

Angela Woodhatch pulled herself up to her full height, which wasn't very tall. "My Graham would've done anything to keep the nature reserve. He wasn't the most organised chap; he would've been the first to admit that, but he'd never sell out. He said he'd consider their proposal, just to get rid of them."

"So you believe because he wouldn't cave in to their threats, they had him killed? Honestly? These are business people, not assassins."

"Who else could it have been? Graham had no other enemies. He was nothing more than a shopkeeper in a seaside town who saw his role in local politics as helping people. And the residents of Redcliff respected him for it. Even if not all of them agreed with his point of view." She lowered her voice. "If you can believe it, there's a movement within Redcliff who actually approve of this development, led by the mayor. She and Graham never saw eye-to-eye. People think it'll bring jobs and prosperity, but my Graham knew what it really stood for."

"Have you told the police your theory?"

"Pah! They say he fell overboard. Graham would never have fallen overboard. They weren't exactly sympathetic when I refused to identify his body. I couldn't. That would be…that would be…"—she held the counter and covered her mouth again—"that would be confirming he'd died."

I faced her and held her upper arms. "Angela, I'll help you find his killers."

"You? What could you do? Are you a private detective as well as a marine rescue volunteer?"

"Um, no. But last month, I helped solve a murder." I squeezed my eyes closed at the thought of doing this all over again, then shook myself. "At least let me try. What else are you going to do? Accept the police's word it was an accident?"

The door banged open behind me, and Emily lurched in. Her ashen complexion betrayed what was still going on inside her, but at least she'd tidied her hair and assembled clothes in a slightly presentable format.

"Are you coping all right, Shiraz? I'm so sorry."

"I'm coping fine, thanks to my new best friend. Emily, this is Angela."

Emily supported herself on the counter and frowned. "We've met before. You come in for a hot chocolate occasionally. But why are you in my kitchen, cleaning my coffee machine?"

"Because I've made coffee, obviously. And I'm about to make more." She addressed two new customers who'd tailed Emily into the *Wicked Whelk*. "Madam, Sir. What can I get you?"

Emily beckoned me, pointed her thumb and whispered. "How did this happen? She's behaving like she owns the place."

"I'll tell you later. For the moment, she's the best thing this morning since sliced bread."

"Apt, very apt." Emily rubbed her temples. "Oh, my head."

"Sit down, and I'll ask Angela to make you a coffee."

Emily groaned and plopped into a chair. "This is all wrong. Me sitting in the *Wicked Whelk,* and somebody else making coffee. It's a horrible dream, and I'll wake up soon."

I laughed. "Would you like anything to eat? A bacon-and-egg sandwich is great for soaking up alcohol. I know how to make them now. Angela showed me."

Oscar pursed his lips. "Angela Woodhatch believes her husband was murdered?"

"Yes. She agrees with your thoughts."

"I didn't say he was murdered."

"No, but you said something wasn't right. You said Graham was an expert boater and was unlikely to have fallen off his boat and drowned."

We sat at Emily's dining table after the café's closing time. At least, two of us did. Emily lay on her couch behind us with a towel and bucket beside her. She groaned sporadically, and Boots didn't help by lying on top of her and vibrating like a purring jackhammer.

I drummed my fingernails. "So you *don't* think anyone killed him, Oscar?"

"I didn't say that either. We don't have enough evidence one way or the other."

"Let's do a mind map again. Emily, d'you have pen and paper?"

"Are we really going to investigate this?" asked Emily. "I don't have the energy today."

"I made a promise to Angela Woodhatch. She's sure Graham was killed, and she's convinced herself the hotel developers did it."

"That's exactly what I said. Case closed." Emily turned towards the bucket and groaned.

"But Johnny Chadwick was presenting to the council meeting at the time of Graham's death."

"He's not acting alone, then." Emily's voice echoed from inside the bucket. "Someone else killed Graham while the meeting was in progress."

"Got it," I said. "Who's the 'Mappin' in Chadwick-Mappin Hotels?"

"His partner, I presume?" said Oscar. "We should write their name down too."

"Yes. Angela told me that someone from the company threatened Graham with the loss of his business. Maybe that was this Mappin person?"

"Where's that pen and paper before we forget these details?"

Emily raised her head from the bucket. "It's in the cupboard under the TV. I would get it for you, but, um, I can't move; I'm cat-disabled. If it wasn't for Angela, I don't know how we would've coped in the café today."

"Perhaps she could help you regularly?" suggested Oscar while I searched the TV cupboard. "It would take her mind off her recent bereavement."

Emily sucked in her cheeks. "Do I need help? I think I can manage."

"You needed help today."

"Today was exceptional. I'm never drinking again."

"Hah," I said, from inside the cupboard. "I'll bet you do."

"Nope. Teetotal from now on. I never want to feel like this again in my life."

I sat back at the table with a pad. "Are we going to do what we did last time, draw the circles with people's names, and lines joining them together?"

"That comes later," said Oscar. "Let's jot the list down first. Start by writing Graham Woodhatch."

"Why? He's the victim."

"He could've committed suicide. Or this really could've been an accident. Don't rule anything out yet. It's too early for that."

I wrote Graham's name at the top of the sheet, followed by 'victim (suicide)?' "Okay. The most likely suspect. Johnny Chadwick. He had the strongest motive." I wrote his name, followed by 'motive—hotel vote'.

"Write down Mappin with the same motive. I don't know their first name, or even if they're male or female."

"What if they paid someone to kill him?" asked Emily.

"Then they're still guilty," said Oscar. "We'll deal with that possibility once we eliminate suspects. Next, let's put down the mayor."

I laid down the pen and furrowed my brow. "Are you serious? I mean, you know her, and we don't, but could she be a murderer?"

"I'm not concluding anything yet. She's friendly with the hotel people. And I'm convinced they bribed her."

"Angela told me they tried to bribe Graham, but he wouldn't entertain their threats."

"So sad," said Oscar. "He would've made a great mayor. An honest politician."

"You're an honest politician," said Emily.

"I've never thought of myself as a politician."

"Next suspect?" I asked.

"Angela Woodhatch," said Oscar. "In every murder, the first person the police interview is always the partner."

"She seemed chipper for someone who recently lost their husband," I said, as I wrote her name.

"Ooh," said Emily from the sofa. "That could be a clue. She's happy he's dead. Maybe she was having an affair? Or they suffered an unhappy marriage, and she stood to benefit financially from his death." She sat up, then held her stomach and lay down again. Boots objected to the disturbance by miaowing, rotating once and snuggling between her legs. "I've got it. Angela Woodhatch was having an affair with Johnny Chadwick, and it was in both their interests to kill Graham. She poisoned his coffee so they could be together, and as a side benefit, the hotel vote would go through. Case closed." She collapsed backwards from the effort of stringing the words together.

"Um, Emily. Graham didn't die from drinking poisoned coffee. He drowned."

"Oh, yes. Sorry, my brain's not functioning properly. I swear I'm never touching alcohol again. Cross off that theory."

"We'll cross items off later." Oscar tapped the paper. "Keep going."

"What about Mr Blakey?" I asked.

"What d'you mean, Mr Blakey?" said Emily. "The pirate? He's been dead two hundred years."

"Oh yes, you weren't there. Well, you were there in body."

"Stop talking in riddles, Shiraz. My brain hurts."

"Last night, at the Smuggler's Tavern, a man met with Oscar and me. He introduced himself as Anthony Blakey and said he was a descendant of the pirate. He also intimated he had a claim to Blakey's Island which would stop the hotel development in its tracks."

"Woah," said Emily. "That's huge. Where did he come from?"

"He found me through my council membership," said Oscar. "He read about the plans for the hotel in the council minutes on our website."

"I'll write his name down for completion," I said, "but he's far too suave to be a murderer. He has such impeccable dress sense."

"What does a murderer look like?" asked Emily. "Anyone could be a murderer. You could be."

"Thanks." I puffed. "D'you want me to add my name to this list?"

"Sorry, I was making the point that it doesn't matter how smartly dressed this Anthony Blakey is, we can't rule him out."

"What would his motive be?" asked Oscar. "He's on the same side as Graham. He doesn't want the development. If he did, he'd never have contacted me."

"True," I said. "Motive as yet unknown. Anyone else?"

"Not that I can think of at this stage." Oscar turned the pad upside down and ran his finger beside our list. "There's something fundamental we should take into consideration. Something about our suspect that means we could identify them right now."

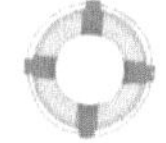

CHAPTER SEVENTEEN

I ran my eyes up and down the list. "What d'you mean, Oscar? What have you spotted that would enable us to pinpoint the suspect?"

"Think about the circumstances of Graham's death."

"He fell, or was pushed, off his boat, into the sea."

"Where was his boat?"

"Close to Blakey's Island."

"Correct. Close your eyes. Imagine you're Graham. You take your boat fishing, something you've done many times before, and someone pushes you overboard. What's missing in between those two events?"

"How did the person who pushed Graham overboard arrive on the boat?" said Emily.

"Yep. What would be the easiest way for someone to board his boat? Think like Graham. Why would you allow anyone to join you on the vessel?"

I drummed my fingers. "Because you knew them?"

"Correct. The chances are, someone Graham knew pushed him overboard. Now we need to work out who."

Murph was yelling into a mobile phone when Emily and I entered the marine rescue shed that Sunday morning.

"What d'you mean, escort them? Terry, we're a search and rescue emergency service, not some kind of marketing prop. Yes, I understand this is important, but I don't want to set any kind of precedent. I didn't complete ten years of training to be a millionaire's babysitter."

We exchanged puzzled glances.

"I know she's the mayor," continued Murph to whoever was on the other end of the line. "That doesn't give her any right to remove my vessel from active service. Whatever next? Will she dial up a police car to take her to the hairdresser?"

Murph nodded a greeting at us and turned away. His broad shoulders slumped. "I don't have any choice, do I? But I'm not escorting them. We'll drive past at normal speed, with no blue lights flashing or anything, so she can point to us and show off her connections to Redcliff Marine Rescue. I'll even ask the crew to wave. Assuming we don't get a shout, Terry. If we receive a call-out, we're going to that. Even the mayor has to understand saving lives at sea's more important than cocktail parties with her developer mates. All right? Bye."

Murph pressed 'end' on his phone so hard I worried he'd crack the screen. He threw the device onto a couch. "Shivering sou'westers. This is the absolute limit. I'm a fully trained search and rescue skipper. I'm responsible for saving over three hundred lives. I've received medals for bravery and, together with other members of our highly qualified crew, I've been presented to the Queen. And now they want me to be an escort boat for a millionaire's yacht. I'd rather resign."

Nooo. Six weeks into my new life as a marine rescue volunteer, and my mentor's quitting.

"Don't do that, Murph," I pleaded. "We appreciate your knowledge and training more than you could know." I beckoned him to the open roller door and pointed out to sea. "Is that the yacht you're talking about?"

A short distance away from the harbour entrance, a large, pristine motor cruiser lay at anchor, gently rolling in the swell. Crew members dressed in white jackets, navy trousers and caps moved around her decks, no doubt preparing for the influx of dignitaries the hotel developers needed to impress. She looked completely out of place here at Redcliff, where the largest craft were the commercial trawlers, covered in rust and adorned with peeling paint. I knew exactly what she'd look like inside, as Montague Jones PR had owned a nearly identical one. I turned my head and smiled to myself as I spied my new favourite boat, the red rescue vessel, bristling with safety gear and without a chrome railing in sight.

"Yep," said Murph. "That white lump's the eyesore. I figured it was lost, or maybe stopped to re-provision on its way somewhere, then Terry called me."

"Terry?"

"The chair of Redcliff Marine Rescue. He's a retired naval admiral. It seems the mayor rang him to ask a favour, and now we're relieved of our usual training responsibilities. Instead, we have to wait for the yacht to moor up, then the council members will board her, and the yacht will take them on some kind of jolly around Blakey's Island."

"What do we have to do?"

"Once the yacht's departed, we're to speed past at full throttle to make it look like we're on the way to a shout. Terry reckons the mayor wants to show the hotel chaps we can deal with any medical emergencies at the island. Personally, I think she's showing off."

"Why don't you simply say 'no' to Terry?"

"She's got him over a barrel. These politicians, they're all corrupt, the lot of them. We have a planning application submitted to extend our building into the car park and enlarge our training and storage facilities. Goodness knows we need to."

"Ah. And the mayor would wave the application through if we keep on her good side?"

"That's what Terry said. If we don't cooperate today, we can kiss the new rooms goodbye."

"That's shocking," said Emily, flaring her nostrils. "It should be on the front page of the papers. 'Mayor threatens to deny emergency service training facility unless they help her pet project'."

"I told him, we'll do one drive past in the middle of training. Nothing else. And if we get a job, we're not even doing that. Ah, hello, David. Welcome to Redcliff Marine Yacht Nannying Service." Murph stomped off to the back of the shed, while David shrugged and gave us a 'what-did-I-miss?' look.

David helped Emily and me perform the kit check before the rescue boat left the harbour. Every piece of equipment had to be present, in its right place and working. As we ticked each item off a list, we gained the muscle memory we'd need if we had to grab something at short notice. I noticed Emily peeking at David from under her cap. He was professional enough not to mention putting her to bed with me the other night.

"Binoculars, Shiraz?" David called from the stern of the vessel.

"Yep. Present in forward port locker."

"Torch times two?"

"Also in forward port locker."

"Working?"

"Just a sec; I'll switch them on. Yep, they're working."

"Spare batteries?"

"With the torches."

"Night vision device?"

"Is this it?" I held up a yellow plastic tube that resembled a short, stumpy telescope.

"That's it. Working?"

"How do I tell?"

"Press the round button on the top and see if there's a glow from the screen. Don't look through it in the daylight; it'll blind you."

"How does it work?"

"Next time we're on night training, ask me, and I'll show you. Earmuffs?"

"Four pairs."

We continued until we'd identified every item on the list and confirmed it all was operational.

Murph stood looking out of the roller door with his hands in his pockets as the white yacht navigated to Redcliff's harbour wall, and the crew tied her up. "At this point, we'd usually power up the rescue boat and head out to sea. But we can't, can we? We can't because Mrs Fancypants Mayor says she doesn't want us to perform that manoeuvre quite yet." He shouted into the air. "I'll tell you what I think of that.

It's a complete and utter insult to everything we've trained for. You can take your yacht and stick it."

"Shh," said Emily. "Here come the council."

"Ppf," said Murph. "If anyone needs me, I'll be brewing a cup of tea. Or do I need to ask the mayor if that activity fits into her little schedule?" He turned away and entered the door to the kitchen.

Emily, David and I watched the council members walk past. The guest list seemed to include their wives and husbands too. Oscar was alone, and I remembered it was Sunday, so his wife would be at church. He rolled his eyes and gave me a subtle thumbs-up as the procession crossed in front of the marine rescue station. Two sailors dressed in crisp, white uniforms welcomed the delegates at the bottom of a ramp leading onto the yacht and steadied some of the older hands. At the top of the gangway, Johnny Chadwick stood with his arms outstretched like a generously proportioned Messiah. As soon as the last guest boarded, the sailors slid the ramp efficiently onto the yacht, untied the lines, and she edged away from the wall.

"The yacht's sailing, Murph," I said, as we entered the kitchen.

"It can dance the polka for all I care. We'll head out and do our civic duty later. Tea's more important."

Murph pressed the kettle's button and tugged a container of biscuits from a cupboard. Boots sat at his feet and stared up at him, as he dropped teabags into mugs, glugged milk and clattered a spoon. I compared Murph's and

Emily's beverage-making skills and wondered what his opinion would be of my usual coffee order.

He sat on the sofa with his mug, broke off a piece of biscuit and gave it to Boots, then addressed his crew.

"First, I want to review our cardinal mark training."

"North, South, East and West," said Emily. "They show mariners the location of safe water."

"Very good. Shiraz, how many flashes does an East cardinal mark make at night?"

Clock face, remember?

I pointed in the air and said, "Never Eat Shredded Wheat," quietly to myself. East was at three o'clock. "Three."

"Correct," said Murph. "Three in a row, then a pause. What makes nine flashes?"

"West," said Emily, before I could respond to the easy question.

"Excellent. Who remembers what a north cardinal mark shows?"

I leant forward. "It's not twelve, then a pause, is it? No. It flashes continually, without stopping."

"Perfect," said Murph. "And a south?"

"Six short flashes and a long one," said Emily, grinning.

"Ten out of ten," said Murph. He sipped his tea. "Now, it gets harder."

Great. That was hard enough.

He showed us a laminated card with four black poles depicted on it. Two triangles were mounted on the top of each pole in four distinct patterns. "What do these cardinal marks look like during the day?"

The one with two triangles pointing upwards must be north.

I was about to point to the first one and shout 'North', when Murph's and David's pagers beeped, and the wail of the marine rescue siren interrupted me.

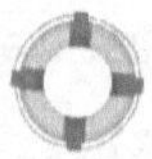

CHAPTER EIGHTEEN

David jumped up, yanked his pager from his pocket and pressed buttons, while Murph tipped his tea down the sink, clomped into the kit room and tugged on waterproofs. Emily and I followed him.

"Strictly speaking," he said, "you two aren't supposed to come on callouts yet, as you haven't completed your qualified crew certificates. But our SOPs, or Standard Operating Procedures, say that if you're already on the boat when we receive a call, you're permitted to be involved so long as you stay within the limits of your training."

I paused. "But we're not on the boat."

"You'd better climb on sharpish, then," said Murph, with a grin. "Get yourselves kitted up."

David entered and pulled his gear from a rack.

"What've we got?" asked Murph.

"Person in the water. Someone fell off the yacht."

"What?" My mouth gaped wide open. "The hotel company yacht?"

"Yep. Quick as you can," commanded Murph. "This is a mayday."

Murph started the engines as David untied the rescue boat, and we zipped between the moored craft towards the harbour mouth.

"What's her location?" I asked. "I'll write it on the log."

"We don't have it. But she'll be easy to find. There's only one seventy-foot yacht in the bay today. Or any day, for that matter."

"Do we know who fell off?" yelled Emily, as Murph pushed the engines to top speed.

"Nope. The Coastguard gave us almost no information."

"I hope it wasn't Oscar. The water'll be freezing."

"There's no way Oscar would fall off a boat," I said. "He's an ex-marine rescue skipper. He wouldn't be so careless."

"Either way, we don't have long to reach whoever it is," called Murph.

"I can see the yacht." I pointed. "Over there."

"I've got her," shouted Murph, "but never say 'over there' when directing me. Tell me where you see it. Port side, starboard side. Bow, stern. Degrees if you can. Or numbers of a clock face."

"Sorry, Murph. Yacht off starboard bow. Two o'clock."

"Better. Thank goodness it's calm today. We'll be beside her in five minutes. Anyone in the water during February needs to be hoiked out quickly before they succumb to hypothermia."

"Like Graham did," I said to myself.

Emily held her right arm out straight. "Object in the water. Directly off the starboard side. Three o'clock."

"Hang on," called Murph, and we all gripped various parts of the vessel as he swung a tight right turn.

"It's orange," I said. "A lifejacket, or a buoy."

"It's a life ring," called David. "And someone holding on to it. Quick, Murph."

"She can't go any faster. Prepare to bring a casualty on board. Grab the foil blankets, regular blankets, anything that'll keep them warm. One minute, and we'll be alongside."

David opened a locker and tugged out a bright-orange foil sheet and a large, red, woollen blanket. He also grabbed a spare lifejacket from behind him.

"Ten seconds," yelled Murph. "Everybody ready?"

"It's Oscar," called Emily, as she pointed to a head and shoulders waving from inside the life ring.

"No!" I yelled. "He's seventy years old. Will he survive this?"

"He's the fittest seventy-year-old I know," said Emily. "Remember, he swims every day with the Redcliff Icebergers."

"Grab under one arm," yelled David. "I'll lift the other."

We pulled a very bedraggled Oscar on board and sat him between us. He spluttered and rubbed his face. David slipped a lifejacket on him by pulling his arms through it, like a parent might help a schoolboy put on a blazer. He wrapped the foil blanket around him.

"Assessment?" called Murph, as the engines idled.

"Conscious and breathing," said David. "Alert, but not communicating with us."

Oscar puffed and blew water from his mouth and nose. He coughed and choked, and I patted him on the back.

He turned to face me. "No need to thump me. I'll live. I swim in the sea every day, remember? This is my second dip this morning."

"Casualty is speaking," shouted David to Murph.

"Keep him warm. Radio the Coastguard and tell them the status. And ask who reported the man overboard. Because that yacht didn't look like it was stopping to pick him up."

"Right-o, skipper." David pushed the button on the handset.

"Coastguard Headland Bay, this is Redcliff Marine Rescue. Over."

"Redcliff Marine Rescue, Coastguard Headland Bay. Go ahead. Over."

"We have the casualty on board. They are in good condition. We are returning to base. Over."

"Good condition?" said Oscar. "That makes me sound like a horse."

We laughed in collective relief at Oscar's good humour.

"Thank you, Redcliff Marine Rescue. Please advise your ETA to base. Over."

"ETA: ten minutes. Please confirm source of mayday call. Over."

"Thank you. We'll revert with that information. Coastguard Headland Bay out."

"We'll head back," said Murph. "Hold on."

Murph pushed the throttles, and we huddled close to Oscar to shield him from the wind and keep his temperature up.

"David," yelled Murph. "Jump on the radio again and request an ambulance meet us at the station."

"I don't need an ambulance," shouted Oscar. "I need hot tea and dry clothes. Maybe a whisky."

"Safety precaution," said Murph. "You know that, Oscar. The paramedics have to check for secondary drowning."

"I don't even have primary drowning." He choked again.

"How on earth did you fall off the yacht, Oscar?" I asked.

"Quite simple. I must've drunk too much Champagne."

We sat in Redcliff Marine Rescue's breakout room. The paramedics had arrived and checked Oscar over, much to his disgust, then proclaimed him in good health and reluctantly accepted his refusal to go to hospital. Meanwhile, Emily popped to his house to fetch dry clothes, and he sipped tea on the couch. No one had yet found him a whisky.

"David," called Murph. "Call up the Coastguard again and find the origin of the mayday call. You can't have someone fall off your boat and keep motoring into the distance."

"I was lucky someone threw a life ring," said Oscar. "I don't know how it happened. One minute, I was leaning over the edge taking a photo with my phone, the next, I was swimming."

"You were even luckier not to have concussion," said Murph. "That's a decent-sized yacht. Falling into water from height can be like hitting concrete."

David returned. "The Coastguard said a private phone called in the mayday. Someone called Mrs Coulston."

"That'll be Sonia Coulston, one of the other councillors," said Oscar.

Murph shook his fist. "At no point did the yacht skipper issue a mayday to alert the authorities he had a man overboard? And he kept steaming away."

"Maybe he didn't know?" I suggested.

"It took us ten minutes to reach Oscar and pull him out. Ten minutes was more than enough for the crew to inform the skipper of the situation. I'm sure this Sonia would have told someone. Probably everyone. She would've yelled. Wouldn't you do that? Wouldn't anyone?" He thumped the arm of his chair. "I'm requesting a Coastguard investigation into that yacht and its skipper. Negligence, that's what it is. Oscar could've drowned or frozen to death."

Oscar grinned. "I'm here to tell the tale. That's what matters. The most annoying thing is, I lost my hat."

"D'you feel well enough to go home now?" I asked.

"Yes, but, Murph, could you spare Emily and Shiraz? My wife's out at a church function, and someone should keep an eye on me, I suppose."

"You're right. Training's over, anyway. David and I'll retrieve the boat. Emily, Shiraz, remove your overalls and escort our casualty home. And if his complexion becomes pale, or if he slurs words or seems disorientated, call the ambulance immediately. Don't hesitate."

"Of course, Murph," I said. "We'll look after him."

Oscar unlocked his front door. We'd been ready to hold his arms on the short walk, but he brushed us off.

"Drink?" he asked. "I'm having a whisky."

"Not for me," I said. "Sit down. We'll fetch it."

"You two sit down." He spoke so forcefully, we obeyed. "You'll need to be sitting down for what I've got to tell you."

"We're sitting down," I said. "Go ahead."

"I didn't fall off the yacht."

Is he suffering from memory loss? Confusion? Should I call the ambulance?

"Yes, you did," said Emily. "We pulled you out of the water."

"I didn't say I wasn't in the water. I said I didn't fall."

"Ooh," said Emily. "D'you mean…?"

"Correct. Someone pushed me."

CHAPTER NINETEEN

Emily and I exchanged glances as Oscar poured a glass of single malt and collapsed into his favourite armchair.

"From the beginning," I said. "Tell us everything."

"Very well. Although I'm not accustomed to being the one on the receiving end of an interrogation." He sipped the whisky. "We boarded the yacht, and immediately they offered Champagne to all the council members and their partners. I'd never seen such a luxurious boat. The flooring was carpet, for goodness' sake. Carpet. Every boat I've boarded had a deck. This had shag pile so thick you could lose a shoe in it. Brass railings everywhere and varnished teak. We took our drinks inside, where more staff stood holding trays of canapes. Chilled salmon, gigantic prawns, thinly sliced beef, vegetarian options, all presented as if they were exhibits in a museum display case. I felt afraid to try anything in case I messed up the arrangement.

"Hah," scoffed Emily. "Posh food. You need to eat about twenty items to get a mouthful. Not like a good, honest, Wicked Whelk toasted sandwich."

"Go on, Oscar," I prompted.

"I didn't intend to drink more than one Champagne, but they topped us up constantly. I realised we'd left harbour when the gentle rocking increased, and I remember thinking what a good job it was a calm day; if it'd been rough, a lot of that Champagne would've ended up over the side."

"What a waste that would've been," said Emily. "Was it Bollinger or Lanson?"

Since when did you become a Champagne connoisseur?

"I didn't see the bottle," continued Oscar. "Regardless, as we headed towards Blakey's Island, I asked a member of the serving staff where the head was."

I furrowed my brow. "The head?"

"It's the nautical term for a bathroom," explained Oscar. "The lavatories. She indicated a corridor towards the bow, so I walked that way and found the facilities, which were more like what you'd find in a five-star hotel than on a boat. Once I'd finished, I opened the door and was about to return to the reception, when for some reason I turned left instead of right. Call it a police officer's, or ex-police officer's, nose for trouble."

"Ooh," said Emily. "This is where it gets interesting?"

"Indeed. Further along the corridor, I came across a room with a glass door. A quick peek revealed a table with what looked like construction diagrams rolled out on it." He paused and rattled the ice around in his whisky glass.

"You opened the door, didn't you?" I said, leaning forward.

Oscar winked. "We're on the same page. I poked my head in to see if I had company, and I was ready with an excuse that I'd mistaken the room for the lavatory. I nipped over and looked at the diagrams. Their title stated they were the plans for the hotel on Blakey's Island."

"The ones the council had viewed, but the public weren't allowed to?" asked Emily. "You'd seen these already?"

"Uh-uh. The plans I'd seen were a subsection of their real intentions; on the table, this diagram depicted an enormous edifice covering the entire island. Most of the rock where the seabirds nest was to be removed, and a vast dome with a glass roof would replace it. Remember the company's other hotels are in tropical locations, and we were surprised they were building one here? This is what they're really up to. The entire resort's going to be indoors. They're even enclosing the beach."

"Wow." I gasped. "It'll look like a huge spaceship's landed in the sea."

"An absolute monstrosity. And a complete annihilation of the nature reserve. I snatched my phone from my pocket and snapped as many pictures of the plans as I could. Suddenly, two muscly arms wrapped around me from behind, and someone's palm covered my eyes. I elbowed and wriggled like anything, but this person was not only a giant, but they were also significantly younger and stronger than me. They pulled me backwards out of the room, kicked open the door to the side deck and threw me over the edge. That's how I ended up in the sea. And I lost my hat but, even more devastatingly, I lost my phone with the pictures on it. The evidence is now at the bottom of Redcliff Bay."

He sighed and ran his hand through his hair. "I've got no proof any of what I just said is true." He drained the whisky and sat back.

"Did anyone see this person throw you over?"

"No one. They were all inside the reception room. Sonia, who rang in the call and must've thrown the life ring, was on deck getting some air. Thinking about it, she told me she suffers from seasickness."

"You were lucky she does," said Emily. "If she hadn't been out there, your absence might not've been noticed until it was too late."

I rubbed my chin. "A random thought. D'you think the person who threw you over was the same person who drowned Graham Woodhatch?"

"What possible connection could there be?"

"You're both on the council, both against the development. Maybe the hotel company's picking off its detractors one by one?"

Oscar raised his eyebrows. "There's a thought. Perhaps I should tell every other 'no' voter to look over their shoulders. This whole incident makes me even more determined to stop this development. They're hoodwinking everyone, possibly bribing the mayor, and now they've tried to drown me. I'm going to use everything in my arsenal against them. And right now, my number one weapon is Anthony Blakey."

I pursed my lips. "We don't have any proof he really has rights to the island."

"Doesn't matter. We can get that later. I'll dig around in the records office in Headland Bay to see if we can link him to the pirate. That'd be a start. We know his name's Blakey from his driving licence, which is half the proof. I'll call him and bring him into our fold."

A weird combination of wariness and excitement shivered through me at the thought of acquainting myself more closely with the pirate's descendant.

"How are you going to contact him?" I asked. "We don't know where he lives."

Oscar plucked a small piece of paper from his mantelpiece and handed it to me. "His business card. Thank goodness this didn't go the same way as my hat and phone."

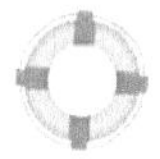

CHAPTER TWENTY

Anthony Blakey sat alone in his accommodation, staring out of the window into the dark.

The waves ebbed and flowed on the shingle below, and he felt a rush of adrenaline as he imagined Shiraz sitting in her home listening to the same ripples.

His plans for Blakey's Island were going considerably better than he could've dreamed.

The ex-warden had agreed to his part of the bargain. But his terms had presented a problem. A solvable problem which took Anthony many days of plotting to fathom out. And the final part of that scheme had yet to eventuate. But it would, imminently.

The retired policeman, Oscar Wainwright, had fallen for the invitation to the clandestine meeting. The one where Anthony revealed his links to the historical pirate, gained his confidence and infiltrated his team of 'no' voters.

'No' to the development of his island.

Alcatraz, Robben Island, Devil's Island. And now Blakey's Island. They all had one thing in common.

He couldn't believe his luck. She'd been there with Oscar. His Shiraz. He'd almost blown everything when they were introduced. She hadn't changed a bit since he'd last watched her from the public side of the red carpet. Even though they met this time in a dingy, low-ceilinged country pub, she still dressed as if she were the centre of attention at a London nightclub. And her smell. Her scent. It transported him back to the only time they'd ever touched, and he hadn't washed her essence off for days.

Oscar had introduced her as his associate. They were on the same team. Anthony had kissed her hand. Kissed her, no less. And now, he was on the team with them. Who knows what might've happened that evening if her idiot drunken friend hadn't interrupted their cosy chat?

But Oscar was sharp. He was looking for evidence which Anthony Blakey didn't have.

The subterfuge would need to continue for longer.

It would have to, if Anthony was once more going to breathe the same air as Shiraz.

CHAPTER TWENTY-ONE

The Wicked Whelk contained a big surprise as I dropped in the following morning to collect my regulation double shot, skinny latte. Emily had, as usual, clumped down the apartment stairs and slammed the front door at 5:30 a.m., and I had, as usual, pulled the duvet up, wiggled my head into my pillow and returned to the land of dreams.

Until 8:30, when my body screamed so loudly for caffeine, I had to respond to its appeals for sustenance, dress in a semi-respectable fashion, tug my beanie hat over my bed-hair and follow her.

Someone stood behind the counter with Emily. Someone I hadn't expected to see.

Angela Woodhatch.

"Here comes a familiar face," she said, as I weaved through the tables of cable-knit-jumpered fishing people and made a beeline for my coffee machine saviour.

"Morning, Emily. And, hello, Angela. I wasn't expecting to see you here again."

Emily grinned as the coffee machine hissed beside her. "Angela said she'll help during the morning rush, which is fantastic. Oscar was right. I need more hands. It's such a struggle trying to prep, make coffee and serve alone."

"As I mentioned on Saturday," said Angela, "I'm happy to work here. It keeps my mind off things. I've had the police swarming over my home looking for anything related to Graham's death, and I need to be out of the house. They even searched my bed. Can you believe that?"

"Does that mean you don't need my help anymore, Emily?" I asked. Because if she didn't, this was a massive relief. My greatest achievement in the café so far had been consuming leftover food.

"Sorry, Shiraz. I, um, know you mean well. But Angela's, er, more..."

"Domesticated?" I laughed. "It's okay, Emily. I'm not offended."

The cable-knit jumper crowd stood, grabbed sea jackets and hats and departed as a throng.

"Tide's turning," said Emily. "That's why they're off now. Take a seat, Shiraz, and I'll bring your coffee."

I plopped down at a recently vacated table and pushed discarded plates and cups to one side.

"Here, I'll take those," said Angela, and she piled up the crockery and cutlery, lifted it and wiped the table all with two hands. It would've taken me at least six.

Emily brought my drink and sat opposite me. Behind us, Angela continued to clear tables.

"She certainly seems to be a great help," I said. "You hardly ever have the time to stop for a morning coffee with me. But I thought you couldn't afford to pay anyone?"

Emily shrugged. "I can't. Angela doesn't want money. She's only helping for the busiest two hours of each morning; says it gives her a reason to get out of bed. I'm happy to do anything to improve her life. Poor woman. This must all have been a terrible shock." She whispered, "And I can't believe Oscar suspects her. She's too friendly."

Angela whistled a tune behind us as she loaded the dishwasher.

I lowered my voice and leant towards Emily. "She doesn't sound very shocked. If I didn't know what happened to her husband, I'd say she seems quite happy."

"I suppose she's putting a brave face on it. Or maybe it hasn't sunk in yet."

"What's your take on the weekend's events, Emily? We haven't had a good chat since that night in the pub."

"Don't remind me. Angela found a bottle of apple cider vinegar this morning at the back of the cupboard, and the sound of the word 'cider' made me feel nauseous again."

I laughed. "I'll bet you're drinking again by next weekend."

Emily gave me a stern look. "Don't, Shiraz. I'll be sick. I mean it."

"Sorry. Moving on. This whole thing with the yacht's terrifying, isn't it? To think these people are desperate enough to throw an old man overboard, and…"

"Oscar's not old."

I blushed. "Ahem. To throw a man overboard, and then lie about what happened. I wish Oscar hadn't lost his phone. I would've loved to see those hotel plans he discovered."

"If Oscar's little scheme with Anthony Blakey comes to fruition, it won't matter what the hotel company's plans look like, they won't be going ahead."

"No. In Oscar's words, that'd throw a vast spanner in the works of the mayor's little scheme."

Emily grinned. "You've met this chap. D'you really believe he's descended from the pirate?"

"I can tell you two things about him. His name's really Anthony Blakey. I saw his driving licence. And second, he's very suave and sophisticated. But in a dangerous way. D'you know what I mean by that?"

"Nope. I don't have a lot of experience with dangerous men. Or any men at the moment, for that matter."

"You were getting on well with David the other night."

Emily covered her mouth. "Please. I can taste the cider just by hearing his name. What d'you mean by dangerous?"

"I mean, he has that aura about him. The aura of trouble. To some women, that's quite intoxicating."

"To you?"

"I'm not sure. But he's bugging me. I'm certain I've seen him before." I shrugged. "Maybe he looks like someone else?"

The door swung open, and a cool breeze heralded Oscar's entrance.

"Morning, Oscar," called Emily. "Have you recovered from your adventure? Black Earl Grey tea?"

"Yes, please. I see you have help." He dragged a chair out and sat next to me. "Is Angela a permanent fixture now?"

"She's helping me in the mornings," said Emily. "It keeps her mind off things."

"We were discussing Anthony Blakey," I said, "and also your dunking at the hands of the property developers."

"Not so loud." Oscar glanced around the room. "Keep this between ourselves. We don't know who's on our side."

As there was no one in the café but us and Angela, I wasn't sure who he referred to, but I took his advice.

The door opened again.

"Here's a chap you wanted to meet, Shiraz," said Emily. She stood and pushed in her chair.

"I did?"

"Yep. Jim Turner. The pirate tours man. I'll make his coffee and bring him over for a chat." She waved at Jim and nipped behind the counter. Steam rose from the machine, and I heard the beans grinding.

"What's your interest in Jim Turner?" asked Oscar, quietly.

"I'm intrigued by his pirate expeditions. They sound fun."

"He's certainly done well out of spinning yarns about Captain Hook-types, smugglers and wreckers. But it's like the Loch Ness Monster, or Bigfoot. An entire industry based on fiction. You know I run the marine rescue gift shop in summer?"

"Yes. You told me that."

"I have a supplier who makes keyrings, tea towels and so on with pictures of the rescue vessel on them. Can you believe he suggested we stock an entire pirate-themed range? He reckoned they'd sell better than the ones with the boat."

I laughed. "From your tone of voice, I presume you didn't accept his offer?"

"Don't be ridiculous. Complete and utter hogwash. How could I stand in the gift shop with a straight face and sell Long John Silver rubbish?"

"Shiraz," said Emily, appearing at our table. "This is Jim Turner, owner of the *Anstruther Pirate* and expert on all things pirate in Redcliff."

Jim shook my hand. Shorter than me, with a ruddy, weathered face, no one would've suspected Jim worked anywhere but on the waves. He grinned and showed a mouthful of brown teeth with several gaps. "Pleased to meet you, lass. Emily were telling me you'd like to join my band of buccaneers."

His accent was full-on pirate, and I wondered if he really spoke like that or whether it was all part of the act.

"I'd love to, Jim. I've heard you spin a good yarn."

"Yarn? Honest pirate, Miss. There be no yarns. I teach history, I do. The history of Redcliff; its proud swashbuckling heritage."

I tried not to laugh. "That sounds interesting. When's your next tour?"

"I run them daily summertime, but we're well out of season now, so there's none scheduled 'til Easter. But if you find a couple o' maties, I'd be grog-filled to organise a private one and hoist th' mainsail for ye."

"I'll come," said Emily. "I'd love to hear your tales, sorry, history."

I glanced over the table. "Oscar? Care to join us? My treat."

Oscar rolled his eyes and laughed. "When were you thinking of, Shiraz?"

"Tomorrow afternoon? Once the café's closed."

"Tomorrow's perfect," said Oscar. "My wife's trying to get me to take her clothes shopping. I need a good excuse."

"Excellent. Does tomorrow suit you, Jim?"

"Wednesday be overcast, fourteen degrees, light breeze from the north," said Jim, studying a very non-pirate mobile phone. "Ideal conditions. Bring warm clothes, a coat and a bottle o' rum if ye like."

"Um, I won't be bringing rum," said Emily. "Where's your boat now? Is it still in the middle of the harbour?"

"Noo," said Jim. "Now it's moored against the wall, so I don't need the little rowing tender to ferry voyagers anymore. Some landlubber called Mr Radish bought it. He wanted to hear my historical account of Blakey's Island, too."

"Mr Radish?" said Oscar. "That doesn't sound like a real name." He laughed. "Are you sure it wasn't Mr Beetroot? Or Mr Carrot?"

"Aarr. Ye be a joker, sir. Honest pirate. 'Twas definitely Radish. He paid me cash. Pieces of Eight. Ha-harr. Shiver me timbers, we'll weigh anchor at five bells of the afternoon watch. Look smart then." He picked up his takeaway coffee and left the café.

Oscar shook his head. "Goodness alone knows what he'll have to tell us on Wednesday. I'll take it all with a huge pinch of salt. Five bells of the afternoon watch, by the way, is 2:30."

"Thanks for that," said Emily. "I don't expect it to be dry and factual, like a school history lesson."

"I'm surprised he didn't invite us to dress up in swashbuckling outfits." I said.

"There's still time." Oscar laughed. "D'you have a moment to catch up at my house? I've arranged to meet Anthony Blakey again, and I'd like to run something by you first."

A film of sweat formed on my hands at the thought of seeing the pirate's descendant again, and my insides tingled. "No problem. I can meet him with you, if you'd like."

"I'll leave you to it," said Emily. "I need to prepare for the lunchtime rush." She cleared our cups and busied herself behind the counter.

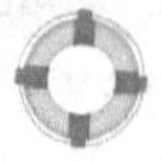

CHAPTER TWENTY-TWO

Oscar tidied papers and invited me to take a seat.

He sat at the head of his dining table with a pad of notes.

"I want to pick your brains," he said. "I need someone to bounce ideas off. Having seen the actual plans for this monstrosity, I'm more determined than ever to stop it, and I know Anthony Blakey's our trump card."

"Agreed. Assuming he is who he says he is."

"Quite. It seems a far-fetched story, and I haven't made time to visit the records office yet, so I can't verify it. Let's work on the basis he is."

I smiled and blinked at him. "Are you sure you're not being taken in by his story because you desperately want it to be true? That doesn't sound like the skeptical ex-police sergeant I know."

"Not at all. But I'm hopeful he's right. And here's how we're going to use him to stop the development. This is what I call 'Operation Blakey'."

Oscar launched into a detailed step-by-step plan, which involved lawyers, the council ombudsman, injunctions and court appearances. His eyes sparkled, and he gesticulated wildly as he explained his intentions. Thankfully, he didn't seem to mention me anywhere in his list of actions, but I wondered if Anthony Blakey knew what he was getting himself into. I zoned out halfway through, and my eyes glazed over.

Oscar finished his speech and slammed the pad shut. "And, at that point, the 'yes' lobby don't have a leg to stand on, and they'll have no choice but to deny permission for the development." He raised two fists above his head. "Victory will be ours."

I stuck out my bottom lip and blew upward. "You seem very certain about this."

"I am. Will you come with me tonight to bring Anthony Blakey up to speed?"

"Um, sure. You'll explain all that again, right?"

"I will. But all we need is for him to represent himself as the legal owner of Blakey's Island. I'll take care of the rest."

Boots sat on one of the marine rescue training room chairs, performing yoga and licking a part of himself I certainly couldn't reach on my body, even with all the Pilates classes I'd attended over the years.

"Shall we sit here, Emily? Boots is saving a row for us."

"Okay. Have you brought your workbook?"

"Um, no. Could I share yours?"

"Yes, for tonight, but if Murph signs us off on anything, clearly you'll need your own."

I sighed. "Yes, I'll bring it next time. What are we learning this evening?"

"Good evening, team," called Murph to the trainees assembled in front of him. "Tonight, we'll revise lights and day shapes. There's an entire computer presentation that goes with this but, as usual, I can't get the laptop to work, so I've given up and slammed the lid closed. We'll use these printed cards instead." He held up an A5-sized flip chart, which made me wish Boots had saved us a seat nearer the front.

"Vessel and danger mark day shapes," began Murph, "come in circles, squares, crosses and triangles."

"This is like Play School," giggled Emily. I smiled and shushed her.

"And the colours black, red, green and yellow," continued Murph. "For instance, if you see a boat with one black circle hoisted, that means it's anchored. We call that one black ball. A vessel in trouble might display two, or even three black balls." Murph flipped the page over to the next diagram.

"So," I said, "the more balls you're showing, the more trouble you're in."

Emily found this *double entendre* funny and bit her bottom lip hard. Boots wasn't quite so amused and yawned so widely I thought he'd dislocate his jaw.

"Well done, Shiraz," said Murph. "You're absolutely correct. Two black balls show your vessel can't be controlled. It's known as being 'not under command'. And three balls indicate you're aground. The most serious situation."

His presentation continued. The sight of black and green triangles, red squares and yellow crosses didn't amuse Emily so much, and she made it to the end without further hysterics.

Murph closed the flip chart. "As tonight's content's short, I thought we'd have some fun. Who knows any Morse code?"

"I know S-O-S." A young man on the opposite side of the room raised his arm. "Dot-dot-dot, dash-dash-dash, dot-dot-dot."

"Very good," said Murph. "That's the only Morse code most people recognise. We no longer train in its use now that we have modern communication methods such as radios and mobile phones. But if you're stranded at sea, your mobile's battery's flat and your radio's dead, it might save your life. Who has a torch with them?"

Everybody glanced around, but no one raised their hands.

"On a boat, you'd carry a torch as part of your emergency equipment, right?" He exaggerated a nod at us. "In the training room this evening, you could use the lights on your mobiles. Let's practice sending each other an S-O-S, one by one. Who wants to go first?"

"I will," said the chap who'd spoken earlier. He switched his phone light on and off in an attempt to make the flashes long and short.

"Could everybody tell which flashes were long, and which short?" asked Murph.

"Not really," I said. "A phone light's hard to turn on and off quickly."

"I'll teach you a trick," said Murph. "This works with any light: a torch, a mobile phone, anything. First, find something opaque. A piece of wood, card, plastic; even your hand if there's nothing else available. Turn on the torch and cover its beam with the item. Then fold your opaque object away from the light and back quickly to make a dot, slowly to make a dash. Tonight, you could either use your hands or your marine rescue workbooks."

He turned to the young man. "Try again."

The man covered his phone's torch with his palm, and we saw three short flashes, three long flashes and another three short flashes emit from the beam.

"Get into pairs," said Murph, "and practice that to each other. Then we'll try something more advanced."

Emily flashed 'S-O-S' directly into my eyes, and I threw up my arm to shield them.

"That works. I can tell you're in trouble, although I might not have any eyesight left to rescue you. My go." I successfully flashed 'S-O-S' back at her.

Once we'd all finished S-O-Sing, Murph handed around a sheet of paper with the letters of the alphabet printed on it, and the Morse code for each letter. "In your pairs, one person sends a word in Morse, and the other translates it. Then swap over."

Emily scanned the page, then flashed to me: dash-dot-dot-dot. I translated that as 'B'. Then she sent three dashes, a pause, then another three dashes. I knew that was 'O' from the S-O-S exercise.

"B-O-O," I said. "Boo?"

"I haven't finished yet." Emily flashed a single dash, then three dots.

"B-O-O-T-S. Boots."

"Correct," said Emily. "Your turn."

"I don't know what to send. Hold on." I thought for a bit, then flashed: dot-dot-dot.

"S" said Emily.

"Correct." I sent: dot-dot-dot-dot.

"Four dots," said Emily, running her finger down her sheet. "H."

"Yep." I flashed: dot-dot.

"That's 'I'," said Emily. "S-H-I. I know: 'Shiraz'."

"Aw, you didn't let me finish." I quickly flashed the letters for 'r', 'a' and 'z'. "Isn't it funny? The first three letters of my name are all dots in Morse?"

Murph glanced around the room at the various flashes popping away. "Has everyone had a go? Take the sheets home, and maybe practice on your family. Especially if you have kids. They love secret codes. You never know when the Morse code might save someone's life." He glanced at the wall clock. "9:00 p.m. That concludes tonight's training, everyone. Thanks for attending. See you next time."

As we stood to leave, Murph waylaid us. "Could I grab you two?" he said. "You may be interested to hear the outcome of your friend Oscar's swimming lesson."

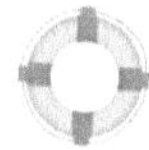

Murph sat us in the breakout room. He made tea, broke a digestive biscuit in half and absent-mindedly handed a piece to Boots, who didn't object.

"The police and Coastguard have spoken with the yacht captain. They're investigating three items. Number one. A passenger fell off the yacht."

"Or someone pushed them," said Emily. I glared at her and tried to shake my head without Murph seeing. Boots miaowed at Murph's feet.

"The police interviewed everyone on the yacht. They rang the guests, none of whom saw anybody fall off the boat. One saw Oscar in the water, thank goodness. I'll come to that. They then interviewed the six crew members and the captain. Two crew independently told the same story; they saw Oscar accidentally drop his phone over the side while taking a picture of the sea. He lunged to grab it and, in doing so, fell overboard. Their stories match exactly, so the police assume that's the correct version of events."

"I suspect collusion," I said, "but go on."

Murph took a sip of tea and fed Boots more biscuit to silence the miaowing. "Number two. Once a passenger fell from the yacht, the vessel in question failed to make a distress call. A person in the water is a mayday, and a commercial vessel by law has to advise authorities immediately. They did not; the call to the Coastguard came from a guest's mobile phone, the woman I mentioned earlier who saw Oscar in the water shouting for help."

"Sonia Coulston."

"That's her name. And number three. Not only did the vessel not call for help, but it continued steaming away from the spot where the casualty had entered the water. Completely reckless behaviour, designed to endanger life."

"I couldn't agree more. What did the captain say about that?"

"He simply maintained that nobody told him anyone had fallen overboard. I find that impossible to believe. Last year, a sailor fell off one of those gigantic container ships some miles off here, and the captain knew about it almost before he'd hit the water. On a seventy-foot yacht, he must've been aware. Or he was asleep at the wheel. Which is another offence."

"Is that the end of it?" I asked.

"Nope. There'll be an official inquiry. But that could be months away. The general feeling in the room, according to my friends at the Coastguard, was this was an accident. Negligence at best. Nobody died."

A gentle swell rocked the *Anstruther Pirate*, and its skull and crossbones flapped in the breeze as Jim Turner stood in the stern, his arm looped around the long, wooden tiller. He would've done well as an extra in a Peter Pan movie; his full-length, maroon coat, silver-buckled shoes, three-cornered hat and patch over one eye complemented his dark complexion and black goatee beard. A belt supporting a plastic sword in a sheath completed the outfit. I wasn't sure he really needed the toy parrot tied to one shoulder, but visiting kids would've enjoyed the whole spectacle.

"Ahoy, me hearties," he announced, as we departed Redcliff Harbour. "Are all ye landlubbers ready for a rollicking voyage into Redcliff's maritime dark side? We'll start with my favourite pirate joke. Why are pirates called pirates? Because they aarrrrrrrr."

Oscar glanced at me from his seat on the other side of the engine, rolled his eyes and grinned.

Emily whispered, "This is going to be great."

Jim Turner had spent years perfecting his act, and even though we weren't his usual day-tripping tourists, I was pleased he hadn't watered it down.

"Aarrrr," he continued. The parrot wobbled as Jim made a sweeping gesture. "This afternoon, our sea voyage will take us to Blakey's Island, the location of much plotting and planning, skullduggery and subterfuge. We'll learn about the arch-pirate Thomas Blakey and his band of fellow brigands, who, two centuries ago, held this stretch of coastline to ransom for twenty long years. We'll hear tales of kidnapping, wrecking, piracy and killing. And we'll investigate the biggest mystery of all." He paused, hunched his back, unsheathed the plastic sword and pointed it at each of us. The effect of his single exposed eyeball staring at us was realistically unnerving.

We hung on his silence, desperately anticipating his next words.

"Aarrrr," he repeated. "The mystery that's kept the good citizens of Redcliff spellbound for nigh on two hundred years. The mystery of Thomas Blakey's treasure."

CHAPTER TWENTY-THREE

"That's the first I've heard of any treasure," said Oscar quietly.

"Ssh." I giggled. "This is fantastic entertainment."

"Show a leg, there," continued Jim, as the boat picked up speed, and we headed towards Blakey's Island. "Sit back, relax and enjoy the ride to the scene of the crimes. The scene of the piracy. The scene, dare I mention it, of the murders."

His voice became slightly less pirate. "If anyone would like to drop a line over the side, this is the part where I invite people to do some fishing."

We all stated catching fish wasn't on our agenda, so Jim reverted to his Captain Hook persona, stood with one leg rested up on the engine mount and steered the tiller with his hip.

The island grew larger ahead of us and, once we'd arrived a short distance off the beach, Jim dropped his boat's anchor, and the chug-chug-chug of his motor ceased. We sat and listened to the water slopping gently against his hull, interspersed with the occasional cries of seabirds.

"Aarrrr," he restarted emphatically, which made me jump. "Here we are, ye scurvy knaves, at the pirate Thomas Blakey's lair. He and his fellow buccaneers lived on board their ship, the *Ruthless Raider*, anchored exactly where we are now." His voice dropped to a whisper. "Seafarers feared this stretch of the coast. Many's a ship's captain's come foul of Thomas Blakey, and lost his vessel on the rocks, to be ransacked, and the cap'n and crew to be sent to Davy Jones' locker."

"Like my hat," said Oscar, peering over the side. "Some modern-day pirate sent my trilby to Davy Jones' locker."

Emily and I leant against the edge of Jim's boat and stared at Blakey's Island. The pinnacles of rock jabbed into the sky above the beach, and the gentle breeze rustled the bushes. "How did he make the ships run aground?" I asked. "Did he board them and threaten the captain at knifepoint?"

"Scupper that," exclaimed Jim. "Navigation aids two hundred years ago were primitive, but effective. In those days, there be a light burning on the cliffs above Redcliff, and another at the harbour mouth. Ship's cap'ns preparing to enter Redcliff Harbour knew, so long as they kept the light on the cliff directly above the light on the harbour wall, they'd navigate their way in safely."

"Leading lights," said Oscar.

"Arrr," agreed Jim. "That's what they be called. The leading lights of Redcliff. Marked on antique charts of the coastline."

"The equivalent of the red and green lateral lights we have today," said Emily.

I laughed. "If only I could remember which side we keep them on."

Emily smiled and turned to Jim. "So what did Thomas Blakey do to wreck the ships? Did he move the lights or something?"

"Aarrrr, that's exactly what he and his ruffians would do. They'd put out the real lighthouse on Redcliff Harbour and make their own one here on Blakey's Island. The ship's cap'ns would believe they were looking at the light showing them the entrance to Redcliff."

"But instead," said Emily, "they navigated by Thomas Blakey's light, and they'd run right up onto the island. And that's where the pirates would capture them and"—she made a dramatic sweeping motion—"slice off their heads."

We all stared at her.

"Um," she said. "I may've read that in an adventure book."

"You're not far wrong, young lass," said Jim. "But Thomas Blakey didn't slice people's heads off. No, indeed. Thomas Blakey would put the boat's cap'n and crew to the sword, and legend tells, he would carve the letter 'B' for Blakey in their chests." Jim demonstrated this with his plastic cutlass, which he pulled from its sheath and drew a 'B' in the air with. "A gruesome calling card, you might say. Dead men tell no tales."

"Blakey was here," said Emily.

"Aarrr," said Jim. "Thomas Blakey was 'ere."

Oscar smirked. "And what, exactly, did Thomas Blakey do once he'd captured the ships? You mentioned some ballyhoo about pirate's treasure."

"Not ballyhoo, sir." He traced an X over his heart. "Honest pirate, it's historical fact. Most of the ships visiting Redcliff carried cargoes from other parts of the country, even overseas. Gold doubloons and pieces of eight, I've no doubt, and Thomas Blakey would've made a good living flogging those goods on the black market. But history tells us Redcliff was an important harbour in those days."

"It certainly was," said Oscar. "Our little town was one of the most significant ports in the country."

Jim's voice dropped again, and we leant in to hear him. "Arrr. Two hundred years ago, the Duke of Redcliff planned for his son to marry a princess from another land far, far across the water." He pointed towards the horizon with the plastic sword. "It was an arranged affair between the titled families, and the couple in question had never met each other."

"Like some foreign weddings today?" asked Emily.

"An arranged marriage," said Jim. "The princess travelled to our country on her father's most magnificent ship, accompanied by an entire court of servants, and chests full of the finest clothes and jewellery. However, it seems in his haste to have her marry our duke's son, and thus ensure a collaboration between their families, the princess's father omitted to have the ship guarded. When Thomas Blakey sighted the princess's ship on the horizon, he would've believed it to be another hapless trading vessel, about to be clasped in his clutches."

We listened, enthralled. Jim's voice dropped further, and we strained to hear him.

"As was their process, Thomas Blakey's men extinguished the light on Redcliff Harbour and substituted their own signal. We can only imagine their glee as the princess's ship ran straight up onto the rocks, right here at Blakey's Island. They boarded her and put the cap'n and crew to the sword." Jim jabbed his plastic cutlass dramatically at me and winked. "Who knows what became of the poor princess at the hands of Thomas Blakey? She, her servants, and her treasure were never seen again. He was a man who gave no quarter. Arrr."

We digested his story. Oscar folded his arms. "If that's true, and I have my doubts, the duke wouldn't have put up with a pirate murdering the princess and stealing her treasure. That must've been the end of Thomas Blakey's reign."

"You be 'andsomely right, sir," said Jim, sheathing his sword and standing upright. "As soon as the duke heard what had befallen the princess, he sent a small army of his best men to capture Thomas Blakey and his band."

"How did they catch him?" I asked. "Did he die fighting the duke's soldiers?"

"They tricked him," said Jim. "The duke's army secretly commandeered an old hulk in another port and provisioned it with rum. One moonless night, they sailed it around to Redcliff. Thomas Blakey, up to his usual tricks, changed the lights, and the vessel was wrecked on the island. But before the ship hit the rocks, the duke's soldiers climbed into a longboat and rowed away."

"So the ship continued sailing into Blakey's Island unmanned?" I asked.

"Honest pirate. Who knows what Blakey and his fellow buccaneers thought when this ship ran aground at full speed in front of them, with no one on board?"

"I'm guessing they didn't care," said Emily. "They just wanted the cargo."

"Aarrrr. The pirates unloaded the rum and being pirates, they consumed several casks immediately, and passed out blind drunk."

"I think I can see where this is going," said Oscar, "but continue."

"The soldiers in the longboat had known exactly what the pirates would do with the rum. After waiting offshore until Thomas Blakey and his ruffians consumed enough to be no danger, they beached the longboat on Blakey's Island, secured the pirates, who offered little resistance in their inebriated state, rowed them back to Redcliff and threw them in the clink."

"Why didn't the soldiers simply kill the pirates while they were drunk?" I asked.

"Arrr. They weren't murderers. It was for the court to pass sentence. Blakey himself was tried for multiple counts of shipwrecking and piracy, and the judge ordered him to be hanged by the neck until he was dead." Jim grimaced and made a gruesome choking motion with his hand under his chin.

"Is all that really true?" I asked. "It seems a bit *Peter Pan*?"

"True, young lady?" Jim gripped the front of his tunic dramatically. "I should make ye walk the plank for that comment. Honest pirate, of course it's true. Everything I've imparted to you today is factual Redcliff history." He 'aaarrred' a few more times for effect. "I hope you've enjoyed today's journey into the exciting pirate history of Redcliff, and the story hasn't frighted you too much. Would anyone like to try for a fish on the journey home?"

"I'd like to try for some hot fish and chips," I said. "It's getting cold, now the sun's setting."

"Good idea," said Emily. "Will you join us, Oscar?"

"Why not? Plus, we need a debrief. I received a call at home this morning. Nothing major, but you might be interested to hear about it. I'll ring my wife and tell her not to worry about dinner for me. Could I borrow your mobile phone, please? Mine's probably directly under us right now."

Emily laid the fish and chips on her dining table and opened a bottle of lemonade. Boots eyed Emily closely and carefully planned his campaign to steal the biggest piece of flaky, white cod from out of its crispy batter without us noticing. I grabbed three glasses and wondered where I could strategically place the lemonade bottle so it didn't tip over and add additional flavouring to the chips.

Oscar divided the chunky, golden chips into three and served them onto plates, sat back and tapped one finger on his mouth.

"Eat up," said Emily. "Don't let it go cold."

"Penny for your thoughts," I said, looking sideways at Oscar. "What's going through your mind?" I passed him a glass.

"Moving parts. Connected happenings. Coincidences. Multiple mysteries." He nodded slowly. "Item one: We have a dead man, who, if he'd been alive, would have voted not to allow a hotel development. Item two: We have the developers, who want the construction to go ahead so badly, they're prepared to throw me overboard to prevent their actual intentions being discovered. Item one and item two are connected. Then, item three…"

"Shall I fetch a pen and paper?" asked Emily.

"Good idea. I'll hold off on item three to let you catch up." He chopped up his fish and ate chips while Emily grabbed a pad and jotted down his first two points.

"Ready," she said, quickly stuffing in fish before Oscar continued. Boots followed her movements with his eyes.

"Item three: Anthony Blakey. He wants the hotel development stopped, although he's very cagey, and I can't discover a rational explanation why. He stakes a claim to Blakey's Island, and his lawyer's posting a document to prove this. This is connected to item one and item two."

Emily scribbled.

"There are other items," I said. "Or maybe they're sub-items. For instance, the boat we saw on Blakey's Island the other week. Did you notice it there today, when we viewed the island from Jim Turner's boat? I looked, and I thought it had gone."

Emily laid down her pencil. "Is that important? I can't see it's connected to any of Oscar's three items. Maybe whoever owned it had collected it, or a storm had washed it away."

"Who knows what's important? The smallest thing could be a clue to this whole mystery."

"Write it down," said Oscar. "We'll cross things out later."

I sipped lemonade. "Then, the strange situation around Graham Woodhatch's death. We know he was an expert boater; we know he always wore a lifejacket and we know it's unlikely he would've drowned. Plus, his widow's convinced he was murdered. She believes the hotel people,

Oscar's item two, were the ones who killed him. They tried to kill you, Oscar, after all."

"And," said Emily, "you noticed his fishing gear was missing."

Oscar placed down his glass. "I'll agree. Something's not right about his disappearance. And the phone call I received this morning confirms it."

"What?" Emily and I asked together.

"I've, um, seen the autopsy report."

"You're such an expert at obtaining confidential information," I said. "I still don't know how you do it. What pricked your ears up in that document?"

"It's very odd. The pathologist concluded Graham had died by drowning, which is to be expected. They also agreed with my summation when I viewed the body that the rocks had smashed his face to the point where it was unrecognisable. But what I hadn't seen, because they'd covered Graham's torso with a sheet, was something strange."

He paused, and we leant forwards. The silence was only interrupted by Boots lapping from his water bowl.

"Someone had carved the letter 'B' in his chest."

CHAPTER TWENTY-FOUR

"Woah," said Emily. "This is spooky. A pirate in the 1700s captured ships, killed the captains and carved a 'B' in their chests, according to Jim Turner's story. Nothing like that's happened since, until Graham Woodhatch turns up dead with the same wounds. But this proves someone definitely murdered him; it wasn't an accident. You don't conveniently carve a letter in your own chest before falling overboard."

My fingernails drummed on the table. "I agree. Could Jim Turner have murdered Graham Woodhatch, carved the 'B' in his chest, then made up that entire story about the pirate two hundred years ago to throw investigators off the scent?"

"He certainly puts on a show, doesn't he?" said Emily. "He remained in character the whole time."

"How much d'you think was true, and how much had he fabricated?"

"He embellished everything," said Oscar. "And some of it had no basis in truth whatsoever. We know there were wreckers in Redcliff who altered lights on shore so ships would run aground. We know there really was a man called

Thomas Blakey, and we know he was hung for multiple crimes, including murder, smuggling and piracy. That much is factual."

"But what about Blakey's calling card?" asked Emily. "The 'B' slashed into his victims' chests. Was that true?"

"Who knows? Pirates could be gruesome. It wouldn't surprise me. All that stuff about the princess and the treasure, that was a fairy story more suited to an animated movie. There was no Duke of Redcliff to my knowledge, and I've heard no one else mention rumours of buried treasure on Blakey's Island. It's a good fable for the tourists."

Oscar laid his knife and fork together. "I'll stake my reputation Jim Turner's not a murderer. I've known him all his life."

"Someone's trying to make a statement," I said. "The mark on Graham's chest was a message."

"To whom?" asked Emily.

"Whoever's investigating his murder."

"Is that us?"

"It shouldn't be," said Oscar. "The police must suspect foul play now."

Emily ran her eyes up and down the pad she'd written on. "These jottings look like a good investigation. Do either of you have any other items we should note?"

"Something's been bugging me." I said. "It's probably nothing."

"What? Any clue could be important."

"Why doesn't Angela Woodhatch seem more grief-stricken? She's there behind your café counter almost cracking jokes. Now and then, I see her sweep her hand over her face, or bite her bottom lip, but I could only imagine that someone who's had their partner's life snuffed out violently wouldn't be able to function at all."

"Ooh," said Emily. "Maybe I have a murderer working in my café? That fits with Oscar's statement that someone Graham knew killed him. She went out fishing with Graham, they had an argument, and she threw all his fishing gear overboard in a fit of rage. Then she pushed him in and wouldn't let him climb back on, so he drowned. Case closed."

I place my fingertips on my forehead and shook my head. "Emily, there are more holes in your theory than in your café's colanders. Angela didn't like fishing, she's a small person and wouldn't have been capable of throwing him overboard and, the final nail in the coffin of your theory, if you'll pardon the pun, at what point in the scenario you've described did she slash his chest?"

"She's still under suspicion," said Oscar. "Remember, the partner's the most likely culprit."

"We already have a list of suspects," said Emily. "We wrote it on Saturday." She riffled through her pad. "Here it is. With Graham himself at the top."

"Cross him off. We theorised that this might've been suicide, or an accident. You can't accidentally carve your own chest."

"Don't cross him off," said Oscar. "Give him a very low score. One."

Emily wrote the number one in a circle next to Graham's name.

"Who's next?" I asked.

"The hotel developers. Mr Chadwick and Mr Mappin."

"And their hired thugs," said Oscar. "The ones who threw me overboard. Give them a top score. Nine."

Emily drew her circle. "Next, Angela Woodhatch. She made the statement someone had murdered her husband long before anyone knew about the mark on his chest. Maybe she was trying to divert suspicion from herself? And, as you said, Shiraz, she seems too happy for a widow."

"People deal with grief in different ways," said Oscar. "She may be in complete denial. But she's definitely a suspect. Give her four."

Emily wrote the number four in a circle next to Angela's name. "And finally, we wrote Anthony Blakey."

"I'd forgotten we'd listed him," said Oscar. "He has to be the most unlikely suspect, doesn't he? He had nothing to do with Graham; had never met him, to my knowledge."

"They are connected, though," I said. "They both want to stop the hotel development. Graham, with his love of the island and the nature reserve. Anthony, perhaps because he wants to claim it back for his family?"

"Give him two. More information needed."

"And we need to add Jim Turner on here. Though I'm not sure what motive he'd have."

Oscar shrugged. "He gets a low score, unless we find out something new."

"We should add anyone in favour of the development," I said. "The mayor, the other councillors who supported it, even you, Emily."

"Me?" Emily froze. "I don't think I want this hotel anymore. Not with what we've learnt over the last week or two. Not now people are dying for it."

I smiled and nudged her. "Jo-king. I know it wasn't you."

"Are we really going to suspect the mayor and half the councillors?" asked Oscar. "If we wrote down everyone who supported the development, fifty percent of the town could be guilty."

"I haven't got enough paper for all of them," said Emily.

"Leave it at that," said Oscar. "If we dilute our investigation too much, we'll miss the actual murderer while we examine completely irrelevant topics. I think our focus should be on the hotel developers and Angela Woodhatch. But we need more information. More clues. Maybe you could subtly interview Angela at work, Emily?"

"I don't want to provoke her into stabbing me with a kitchen knife."

"Hardly likely," said Oscar. "Even if it was her, people who murder their partners aren't generally serial killers."

I paused with a chip halfway to my mouth and gazed into the distance.

"What are you thinking?" asked Emily, staring at me. "Something's going on inside that pretty head of yours."

"Could we land on the island?" I asked. "We might find something which narrows our search."

Emily grinned and jumped up. "I knew it. You can't help yourself, can you? You can't stand to see a loose end untied."

"It's a nature reserve, remember?" said Oscar. "No-one's allowed to set foot on it."

"If the plans you saw on that yacht are correct, the nature reserve's toast. Finished. Every film star and their dog'll be landing on it. I'm going to find a way."

Redcliff Marine Rescue's metal doors were rolled up the following day, and they rattled as the sea breeze gusted through them. The southerly wind brought a rough sea with it, and waves whumped against the sea wall.

After grabbing my morning double shot, skinny latte from Emily, I entered the boat shed and found Murph at the rear of the vessel with the lid of one engine removed, and a set of spanners scattered over the floor.

"Morning, Murph," I shouted from a distance. I didn't want to surprise him.

His bald, bearded head poked up. "Who's that? Oh, hi, Shiraz. What brings you here today? Training's not until the weekend."

"I noticed the shutters open and popped in to say 'hello'. I live next door, remember? What are you up to?"

"There's a problem with the steering. Bubbles in the hydraulics. And d'you think I have a spanner the right size? Someone borrowed the correct one, and I'm having to use an adjustable wrench. Not ideal."

"Will she be off the water for long?"

"Nope. I'll have her fixed this morning. With this weather, we're unlikely to get a shout. Unless there are walkers cut off by the tide. If that happens, the Coastguard'll have to deal with it."

"Do you need to take her out to test your repairs?"

"Test my repairs?" He stood back from the engine and gestured with his right arm. "Would you perhaps like to inspect my work, to confirm I'm doing this right? I've only been fixing our engines for ten years."

"No, sorry, I didn't doubt your mechanical ability. I was wondering if you were planning a trip?"

"Not this side of Sunday's session. Why?"

Out with it. Stop beating around the bush.

"I want to land on Blakey's Island."

"You can't. No one can. It's a nature reserve. Off limits. And besides, that wouldn't be the correct use of the rescue boat."

"Perhaps we could make it part of training on Sunday? Practise landing there, in case we ever have to?"

"There are plenty of beaches we're allowed to land on. West Cove, East Beach, Golden Beach. Why d'you want to land on Blakey's Island specifically?"

"Um, to investigate that tender we saw pulled up there? Maybe the person who's lost it wants it to be towed back?"

"Nope. Redcliff Marine Rescue does not do salvage jobs. We only rescue lives. Not property. Unless a boat's adrift, like that Graham chap's the other week. That was a shipping hazard, so the Coastguard asked us to bring it in. But we never pull boats off beaches."

"Oh. So we can't go to Blakey's Island?"

"We can go to it. We can't land on it. Now, if you'll excuse me, I have to finish this engine and then give my day job some attention. I'll see you at training on Sunday."

"Um, yep. See you then."

I stood outside the boat shed and gazed at the vessels bobbing up and down in the harbour. On this stormy day, the commercial trawlers had departed for the fishing grounds, but the day tripper boats and private sailing craft rocked back and forward with their covers on, their owners sitting indoors waiting for the wind to drop.

I set off for a walk around the sea wall surrounding the relative calm. Outside the harbour, the waves crashed, and foam flew over the stone breakwaters. Inside, the sea behaved like when you carried an almost-full cat's water bowl. Slopping from side to side, but not violent enough to spill. I tugged my Burberry jacket around my ears and felt the salt spray sting my cheeks. As I approached Jim Turner's boat, I found him aboard, busy fixing something in his own engine.

"Morning, Jim," I called. "No customers today?"

He looked up. "Hello," he yelled back, then remembered to slip into character. "Shiver me timbers. My saucy crew from yesterday. Are you returning for more swashbuckling?"

I laughed. This guy really invested effort in perfecting his craft. "You should be in the Redcliff Amateur Dramatic Association. I love your pirate act."

"Act, Miss? Honest pirate. This is no act. I'm the last remaining buccaneer in Redcliff. Ha-harrrr."

"Would it be possible for your pirate ship to give me a lift to Blakey's Island?"

"Arrrr. You liked the trim of her jib yesterday, and you want another ride?"

"Yes, but this time I want to land there."

"Arr," he said, regretfully. "Even modern-day pirates mustn't land on Blakey's Island. Nobody can."

"D'you know anyone who could rent me a boat?"

"In the summer, yes. There are rowing boats for hire. But they're heaved out of the water in the off season."

"Oh, okay. Thanks, Jim."

"Arrr. Good sailing, fair maiden."

I'm not exactly fair, but thanks.

A metal bench with a wooden, slatted seat formed an excellent spot to reflect, and I perched on it, gathered my coat around my legs and watched the gulls soar and cry above the harbour. The cool sea breeze kissed my face and, while I wouldn't have objected to it being several degrees warmer, I loved the feeling of being outside, the taste of the salt air, the slap-slap-slop of the water against the fishing boats. My chest tingled; I knew I'd never felt more alive.

Alive.

Being alive was so good.

I caught sight of Graham Woodhatch's boat, unloved at its mooring.

Graham Woodhatch.

Not alive.

Not so good.

Oscar thought highly of him, which was enough for me to have positive thoughts about the man. I'd never met him, and I didn't know what he looked like, but I'd formed a picture of him, the way you do when you receive a partial description of someone. Black, curly hair, short and plump, ruddy cheeks and a friendly, uneven smile. That was Oscar's description of him. And his personality? A disorganised man, a dreamer, not entirely reliable but his history with the island meant he was very keen to stop the development.

Was that what caused his death?

What about his fishing shop? Could that've been in financial trouble?

And the mystery with his boat, adrift off Blakey's Island. With none of his fishing gear on board.

Blakey's Island. With the mysterious little wooden tender we'd seen, dragged up into the trees. Which then subsequently vanished.

Blakey's Island. An uninhabited nature reserve. Soon to be inhabited by a motley crew of construction workers, tailed closely by film stars and politicians.

Blakey's Island. Out of bounds to everyone.

Murph wouldn't take me there.

Jim Turner wouldn't take me there.

Someone had to. Someone could be persuaded.

I pushed on the arm of the seat, puffed out my cheeks and stood. Time to return home. My preparations for a second meeting with the dark, intriguing Anthony Blakey required some thought.

CHAPTER TWENTY-FIVE

Oscar led me to a deserted wooden hall down a back lane behind Redcliff High Street where a sign said, 'Redcliff Rotary Club'. I knew Oscar was a Rotarian, so it didn't surprise me when he produced a key and unlocked the door. We entered, and he switched on the lights.

"Brr." I hugged myself. "Does this place have any heating?"

"Wait a moment." Oscar flicked a switch on the wall, and an industrial sound in a back room preceded warm air flowing through vents in the floor.

"This is the only place we're guaranteed not to be disturbed," said Oscar. "Ah, here's Anthony Blakey."

As soon as he walked in, I looked away. Then I realised that wasn't very professional and forced myself to smile. I couldn't decide how to feel about him. Was he exciting, or was he dangerous?

"Good evening, Mr Blakey," called Oscar. "Welcome to Operation Blakey's campaign HQ."

"Mr Wainwright, thank you for inviting me." He turned to me and took my hand. "Ms Jones. This is an unexpected pleasure. Your presence perfects the occasion."

He held my hand in his and stroked it. I involuntarily stepped back.

"Please," said Oscar. "Take a seat."

We sat around a small table, and Oscar produced his pad from his briefcase. I stared at his handwriting with resignation that I'd have to listen to his entire presentation again.

Yep. Every word.

Oscar ran through each page, step by step. I glanced at Anthony. He didn't seem interested in Oscar's proposal, and instead fixed his gaze on me. I met his eyes, then looked away.

Oscar closed his pad for the second time that day. "And that, Mr Blakey, is where you come in. One gap I have in this strategy is your document proving your claim to the island. Do you have it?"

"No."

"Where is it?"

"I'm not going to carry such an important artefact around in my coat pocket, am I? My lawyer's keeping it safe."

"Who's your lawyer? When can we see it? Or a copy of it?"

"All in good time. All in good time."

Oscar laid his pen down. "Mr Blakey, we urgently want to use your proof of ownership to bolster our case. But without that document, we have nothing."

Anthony thumped his fist on the table and leant towards Oscar. "Do you doubt me? Are you calling me a liar?"

His voice changed as he raised it, and a less-cultured accent crept into his vowels.

"Calm down," I said. "No-one's calling you anything. Could you bring the document next time?"

He rolled his eyes and inhaled deeply. "Fine. I'll contact my lawyer tomorrow morning, ask him to send a copy immediately by courier, and we could meet in the evening. Does that satisfy you?"

"Tomorrow evening doesn't work for me," said Oscar. "It's the regular monthly council meeting which I can't miss. I'll discover more details about the proposal and hear the feedback from the yacht trip. Although I'm sure my inadvertent ducking will be the principal topic of conversation."

I took a deep breath and half-smiled at Anthony. "I'll collect the document from you tomorrow evening."

"That would be delightful, Ms Jones. I'm so pleased we'll be working together." He paused and flashed me a smile. "You're a marine rescue volunteer, aren't you? And you live at the Wicked Whelk?"

How do you know so much about me?

"Um, yes to both."

"May I propose we meet outside the rescue boat station at 6:00 p.m? That'll be a convenient location for you and give plenty of time for my lawyer's courier to reach Redcliff."

"A perfect arrangement," said Oscar, before I could object. "Thank you for coming today, Mr Blakey. And remember, not a word about this to anyone."

Anthony stood first. He gathered his coat and silk scarf, kissed my hand again, shook Oscar's and departed. I wiped my hand on my jeans and vowed to wash it as soon as I reached home.

"He seems a very professional man," said Oscar. "A delight to work with. I had my doubts, but he's proved his identity and, once we get hold of this document, it's full steam ahead with our Operation Blakey. The mayor and her developer friends won't like this one bit."

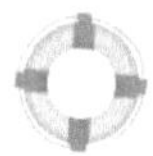

The following evening, I stood in front of the mirror trying to decide whether to wear flats, wedges or boots to meet Anthony alone for the first time. I couldn't work him out. He seemed very interested in me, which felt flattering, but my senses were heightened in his presence. Something about him unnerved me. His eyes. His stare. Plus, I was convinced I'd met him before, possibly only briefly, and I prided myself on never forgetting a face. Perhaps he worked for a client of my ex-husband's? Maybe he was involved with one of the film premieres I'd attended? Maybe he'd been a paparazzi photographer in a previous career?

I jumped, as the sound of 'Dancing Queen' by Abba echoed up the stairs from the street, followed by the slam of the front door.

"Hi, Emily," I yelled. "Did you get everything you need at the wholesaler?"

"Hi, Shiraz." The volume of music coming from her phone reduced, and she popped her head around my bedroom door. "Yes, thanks. I had a successful trip. And on the way home, convertible top down, music up as usual, I came to a decision about myself."

"You did?" I faced her and placed my hands on her shoulders. "What decision is this? What earth-shattering revelation will you impart to me?"

"I'm going to change."

"What, your clothes? Your hair?"

"Both. And my personality."

"Really? I like you the way you are."

"And I like you the way you are, Shiraz. You're an inspiration. A role model. I'm no longer going to be Emily, the stay-at-home, cat-loving, book-reading introvert."

"You're not?"

"Nope. I've been clothes shopping for something revealing and racy."

"Emily! Are you sure about this?"

"Yep, I enjoyed myself so much the other night, drinking Champagne with you, then chatting and"—she blushed and glanced at her feet—"flirting with David and his friends. I want to do it again. I'm going to ask David for a date."

"Gosh. This is a surprise."

Emily clenched her teeth and grinned. "I know, right? Could I borrow your hairspray and GBH straighteners?"

I laughed. "GBH? You mean GHD? Good Hair Day, not Grievous Bodily Harm. Of course you can. Now?"

"Yes, please. I'm going to spend an evening in front of the mirror with the music up, testing hairstyles. Would you like to join me? I bought Champagne." She pulled a bottle from her shopping bag and waved it back and forward in front of my face.

"Champagne? I thought you were never drinking again. Um, sure. D'you mind starting without me? I have to meet Anthony Blakey at the marine rescue building to collect a document, but I'll only be ten minutes. Pour a couple of glasses, and I'll be right back."

I nipped into my bedroom, sat on the bed to pull my shoes on and decided to wear the boots. The sound of a cork popping, and liquid being poured was followed by 'I Will Survive' blasting from Emily's bedroom at high volume. A quick peek around the door revealed Emily wearing a long, cream T-shirt standing in front of her full-length mirror singing into a microphone which one minute ago had been a hairbrush. I laughed as I clumped down the stairs and wondered if 'role model' was the correct moniker for someone who'd introduced her quiet, unassuming friend to the wonders of Champagne and discos.

A fork of lighting jabbed at the horizon as I closed the door behind me and, from childhood habit, I counted the seconds until a distant crack of thunder sounded. I could still hear Emily's music thumping upstairs, and wondered whether the neighbours might complain. Then I remembered the only neighbours were the Wicked Whelk café downstairs, which was closed, and belonged to Emily anyway, and the marine rescue building, which was uninhabited at this time on a Wednesday.

I walked the thirty steps from Emily's door and stood with my back to the roller shutter, which concealed the red rescue boat safely on its trailer, poised to deploy at a moment's notice to rush to the aid of mariners in distress. My chest swelled knowing, one day, as soon as I'd qualified, I'd be one of those people doing the rushing. I took ten steps forward and stood on the harbour wall, staring at the sea.

Another lightning flash lit up Blakey's Island, which formed a distant silhouette, the jagged edges of the rocky crags clearly defined. Puffins sleep at night, don't they? They'd be safely snoozing in their nests, or whatever they lived in, unaware of the turmoil that was about to be foisted upon them if this hotel development obtained approval. And what else was on Blakey's Island? Maybe a clue to Graham's death? My efforts to land on it hadn't come to fruition, and I wondered if they ever would. Drops of rain began to fall, the kind of rain which soaks you even though it's not heavy, and I hoped Anthony would arrive before my hair resembled seaweed.

COUGH

I jumped and swivelled.

"Ms Jones?"

Anthony Blakey leant against the side of the marine rescue building. The side away from the streetlight, so he was in shadow.

"Anthony?" I peered into the darkness. "Is that you?"

The figure stepped forward, and I smelt his musky aftershave.

"Ms Jones. Such a pleasure. My heart can never tire of the glint of light on your hair, the sound of your voice, the scent of your fragrance." He took my hand and brushed his lips against it.

I snatched it away and stepped back. "Do you have the document for Oscar?"

"I do, but it isn't here. Please, come with me, and I'll give it to you."

"Where is it?"

"Where else would it be, Ms Jones, but on my island? Allow me to escort you there, and I'll hand it over."

"Your island?"

"Blakey's Island. My island, as you'll see from the document. My boat's tied against the harbour wall. We'll be there and back in a jiffy. Here, let me help you on board."

I glanced down at the craft he proposed to convey us in to Blakey's Island, a small, wooden, open boat with a tiny outboard engine clamped to the stern. Over my shoulder, the light from Emily's window shone onto the harbour wall, and I heard the muffled thump-thump-thump of her music.

I desperately wanted to reach Blakey's Island, and here I was being offered a ticket on a plate, but...

But something was very wrong, and I trusted my intuition.

"If you've got the document on the island, Anthony, you don't need me to come with you. I'll wait here, and you can motor over and fetch it."

"You have to come with me, Shiraz. You must." He grabbed my wrist and pulled me towards the boat. "We need to go to Blakey's Island together. If we don't, my entire plan will have been for nothing."

I tugged my hand away, and Anthony Blakey responded by grabbing me around my waist and pulling my arm behind my back.

"Shiraz, darling, why do we have to do this the hard way?"

"Help!" I screamed. "Emily! Someone. Help!"

CHAPTER TWENTY-SIX

I raised my heel and kicked my assailant somewhere. I'd no idea which part of his anatomy my boot had connected with, but he grunted and twisted my arm harder. A metal blade pressed against my throat as he dragged me towards his boat and shoved me into it. He kept the knife visible as he pushed a button to start the outboard engine, and a flash of lightning revealed it to be a cutlass, an authentic version of Jim Turner's plastic toy.

"This could've been so much more pleasant," said Anthony. His voice had changed, and the refined gentleman who'd presented himself to me and Oscar had vanished. My body trembled, and I whimpered as cold sweat broke out over my face.

"It was always you, Shiraz," he continued. "You're the only one I've ever loved. I need you. And I know you need me. We'll be happy together, on our own island, for the rest of our lives."

The little boat, my prison ship, motored towards the harbour entrance. I opened my mouth to yell for help again, but crying out was futile; Emily's personal disco continued to boom from her window, interspersed with booming thunder as the storm intensified. The craft rode over the swells, Anthony in the bow, me in the stern. I had a random thought of how romantic this scene would've been, were it not for the sharp blade pointed at me and the cold sweat pouring down my brow. The rain became heavier, and I pulled my lapels around my face.

"You're the only one I've ever wanted," he said. "I can't live without you. And now I won't have to."

He turned away from me to watch where he steered, although he kept the knife aimed at my chest. If I could wiggle my phone out of my inside coat pocket, I could call for help.

Damn. He saw.

"Don't think of trying to escape, my dearest Shiraz. When I show you the life we'll have together, you'll be glad you stayed with me. We're here. Blakey's Island. Our island. Our new home."

The boat scrunched on the beach. Anthony leapt out to tug it further up the sand and, as he did, he slipped in the shallows.

This is my chance. Now or never.

I pulled the phone from my pocket and jabbed at the only button my shaking fingers would connect with.

Redial.

The ringing tone sounded as I held it to my ear.

Come on, come on. Answer. Please. Please. Please.

Tears welled in my eyes, and I let out a huge breath as someone picked up.

"Hello? Emily speaking."

A hand reached from behind me and snatched the phone.

"You won't be needing anyone else, now we have each other," said Anthony, and I watched with horror and anger as he spun my iPhone into the sea, where it splashed twice and sank like a flat stone skimmed across the water by a child.

The knife was at my throat again. "Take my hand, darling. I'll carry you over the threshold."

"You will not," I yelled at him. I stepped onto the sand without his assistance. It was a minuscule gesture, but I wasn't going to let him have the satisfaction of pretending he was my new husband.

"You're so feisty," he said. "We'll have so much fun together. I can't wait for our new lives to begin."

"The only new life that'll begin will be your life in prison."

"There's no need to use words like that, my dearest. I've spent so long preparing for this moment. I'll provide everything you'll need for our nuptials. A fresh wardrobe, with clothes in the colours I love to see, new shoes, the stunning red ones which look so perfect on you, and whatever makeup and perfume you desire. Just say the words, and I'll provide. Oh, and I must buy some groceries for our wedding breakfast. Champagne, too. Bollinger's your favourite brand, isn't it?"

"You're insane. Even if I wanted to, we can't live here. This is a cold, uninhabited rock with nowhere to sleep, or eat, or anything."

"Here. Let me show you." Anthony marched me at knifepoint through the bushes at the back of the beach, removed a torch from his pocket and unlocked the door of a wooden shack. A background smell of stale smoke greeted me, which immediately transported me back to a time sitting on my grandfather's knee in his garden, his pipe wedged firmly in the corner of his mouth. A bare mattress lay on a rusty, metal bed frame, with a stained duvet bundled on top of it, devoid of a cover. Against the walls, a rickety free-standing closet stood alongside a chest-of-drawers. I couldn't see any windows.

"The old warden's residence," he said. "I'm having it refurbished, and we'll make our marital home here. I can't wait to settle down with you."

"I'm not settling down here, you waste of oxygen," I said. "You won't get away with this. Kidnapping's a serious crime. My friends will already expect me home and wonder where I am."

He leered at me, and my skin crawled. "And where will they look for you? Here, on our island, where no-one's allowed to land? That'll be the last place anyone searches."

I panted, and realised he was right. Nobody would find me on Blakey's Island. The time had come to fight back. I elbowed him in the face and heard the satisfying sound of the knife clattering on the wooden floor. Anthony's torchlight darted around as he searched for it and, as the blade reflected in its beam, I kicked it away, grabbed it and pointed it back at him.

My hands shook. "Get away from me. Get away. I hate you." I jabbed the knife at him like I'd seen pirates do in movies.

He held his chin where my elbow had connected and laughed at my efforts to scare him. "You have no idea who you're dealing with, Shiraz," he said, as he backed away from me. "I'm not who you believe I am. You're trapped here, and you're mine. You may have won this battle, but I'll return when you least expect, and you won't escape. Ever." He reversed away from the cabin down the beach, keeping his eyes on me and the torch pointed in my direction.

"My friends won't give up until they find me." I yelled from the cabin door, as I felt my entire body tremble. "They knew I was going to meet you tonight. You're finished."

"Finished, darling? We've only just begun." The torch extinguished as he pushed the boat away from the sand and started the engine. Lightning illuminated it amongst the driving rain as he motored away.

I dropped the knife, slumped to the ground with my head in my hands and bawled.

Kidnapped.

Stranded.

Stranded on an uninhabited island, and no one knew I was here.

Cold.

So very cold. And wet through.

The storm had abated, and a full moon bathed Blakey's Island beach in a stark, white light which illuminated the sea between me and the mainland. The lights of Redcliff twinkled across the water, and I could make out the dark marine rescue station and beside it, the outline of the Wicked Whelk. They could've been on Mars for all they could help me. The square light from Emily's window punctured the silhouette, and I imagined her dancing around her room, trying on new clothes, using up my hairspray. I bit my lip as I realised I might never see my friend again. I couldn't call her. I couldn't call anyone. Anthony had thrown my phone away.

Could I swim that distance? As a teenager, I'd won the eight hundred metre medal at Thornhill Grange Ladies College. I knew Blakey's Island was two miles offshore. But it looked closer. I marched to the water's edge, where the ripples gently lapped, and stuck my flat hand in the shallows.

Icy.

If Graham Woodhatch hadn't been able to survive falling overboard here, there was no way I'd live long enough to cross the strait.

My foot tripped on something solid, and I bent to pick it up. Was that Anthony's torch? It must've fallen from his pocket while he climbed back into his boat. But would it still work? I turned it over, found the 'on' button and pushed it. Yes! A dim, yellow beam shone from the lens. I pointed it directly at the lights of Redcliff, covered the end with my hand as Murph had taught me and began flashing its beam. Three shorts, three longs, three shorts.

S-O-S.

I signalled again and again, then turned the torch towards my eyes and stared into it.

Who was I kidding? No one would see the weak glow from two miles away. I needed to find something else. Maybe Anthony had left a more powerful light in the hut? This seemed unlikely, but I had to cling onto any thread of hope. Because I knew one thing from reading true crime books about kidnap victims.

The longer you remained captive, the less likely your chance of escape.

I had to flee this island before he returned.

The hut door creaked as I swung it open and shone the torch inside. Beyond the room with the bed and cupboard, a door led into a second room at the rear. Devoid of furniture, this contained timber, carpentry tools and unopened paint tins. Sawdust covered the floor.

There must be something in here to help me. Anything.

I returned to the bedroom and flipped over the duvet, but nothing useful hid between it and the brown-stained mattress. Inside the closet, a row of clothes hung from a rail. Men's clothes. Shirts, trousers and waterproof jackets. Below them, two pairs of strong boots rested on the base of the cupboard. I had a moment of hope when I noticed a shelf at the top, and I stood on tiptoes to shine the torch into it, but this revealed nothing but spiders. I allowed myself a small smile as I imagined Emily making this discovery, screaming in fear of the creepy crawlies and running away.

Emily.

Was it only an hour ago when I'd told her I'd return in ten minutes? She must be worried sick. Or maybe she'd become too focussed on her music and dress-ups and had forgotten the time.

Was anyone looking for me?

I turned my attention to the chest. Four drawers, two full-length and two smaller ones above them. The left-hand drawer contained men's underwear, a cheap supermarket brand. In the right drawer, I found thick, tan-coloured woollen socks in various degrees of holiness. The middle drawer enclosed men's singlets, which had been white in a previous life, and the bottom drawer revealed thick jumpers. I presumed these belonged to my kidnapper, although the garments seemed large for his slim build. I wondered how long he'd been living here. At least that explained the little boat coming and going but, as I stood back and wondered what on earth I was going to do next, I realised something.

Anthony couldn't have been living here full time. He'd presented himself to Oscar and me as a suave, dapper gentleman, with a neatly trimmed beard and immaculately styled hair. Nothing in this room betrayed that persona. I'd found no smart clothes, no business shoes, no aftershave. He must have a base on the mainland as well. So why were these dirty, old clothes here? Was Anthony doing the carpentry? His palms were soft, and he had perfectly trimmed fingernails. They certainly weren't the hands of a tradesman.

I licked my lips around the insides of my cheeks, which were as dry as sandpaper. When this was the warden's home, did it have any running water? I turned the taps in the rear room, but nothing came out. Maybe there was some kind of rainwater tank? Time to look behind the hut. What else was I going to do? I had to find a way to escape.

Once, there must've been a clear, neat path to the rear of the ramshackle building. Lush, tangly vegetation had invaded, but the cracked concrete was still visible. I pushed bushes and tree branches to one side and shone the torch through the undergrowth. What was I doing, fumbling around in the dark? What did I hope to achieve? I should sit on the beach, wait for Anthony to return and accept my fate. Or maybe I could surprise him, and overpower him?

I was about to give up on my search for anything useful behind the hut when I tripped, fell and grabbed the nearest object to save myself. I thought it was a long, straight branch, but it felt odd, like it had wire wrapped around it. It was definitely human made.

A fishing rod?

Multiple fishing rods leant against the back of the hut, surrounded by large, plastic containers. I unlatched the clips of one box and found it full of hooks, floats and other fishing paraphernalia. A net on the end of a long pole lay alongside them.

Could this be Graham Woodhatch's fishing gear? Had Anthony murdered him and taken his equipment? Or had he found Graham's boat adrift, stolen the rods and left the vessel for Marine Rescue to find?

None of that seemed likely. Maybe this wasn't Graham's gear at all? Maybe Anthony lived here and caught fish.

I shivered and pulled my coat around me. Nothing here would help me. It would take more than fishing kit, old clothes and a torch to reach safety. I needed to explore further, and hope to goodness this island contained something more useful. It was that, or sit in the hut until Anthony returned.

I strode out of the bushes and marched down the beach. The scene hadn't changed. The moon had moved in the sky, but it continued to illuminate the calm sea, and lights on

Redcliff seafront continued to twinkle. And I was still stuck here on this stupid island. I shoved my hands in my pockets and walked along the sand to the other end. Nearer to Redcliff. Further from the hut.

Rocks.

Bushes.

The smell of seabirds.

Nothing that could be remotely useful to aid my escape.

Nothing that could summon assistance.

I reached the end of the beach and gazed along the small promontory to where the west cardinal mark flashed, marking the rocks. If this light had been present two hundred years ago, the real Blakey's pirate career would never have succeeded.

Nine flashes, then a pause. Nine flashes, then a pause. Repeatedly. All night, whether or not anyone was present to see it.

Nine flashes.

I clenched my fists and jumped up and down on the spot, as I realised exactly how I'd attract attention.

CHAPTER TWENTY-SEVEN

I sprinted back along the beach and thanked the Gods of fashion I'd chosen to wear boots and not heels. The torch dimmed, and I raced as fast as I could to the hut. My life depended on that torchlight for at least a few minutes. I shoved through the bushes at the back of the hut, shone the weak beam on the fishing gear I'd found and grabbed the long-handled net. The hut door squeaked again as I barged in, threw open the closet and wrenched out a waterproof coat. As I ran back towards the cardinal mark with the net and the coat, the torch extinguished completely. I threw it to one side. It had served its purpose, and I could finish my plan without it.

At the end of the beach, I propped up the long handle and zipped the rain jacket around the end with the net. I waded through the rock pools at the promontory, carrying my new tool, my saviour, in two hands. The water covered my boots and soaked the bottom of my jeans, but I had no choice. Short-term pain. Anything to get off this rock.

I reached the west cardinal mark, which continued to emit its pattern of nine short flashes. I held the pole up, and the jacket wrapped around the net obscured the light. Yes! I'd disrupted the nine-flash sequence. All I had to do was make it shine: three shorts, three longs and three shorts.

S-O-S.

Someone in Redcliff would see my signal, and hopefully know what it meant.

Except, at that point, I realised the cardinal mark could only shine short flashes.

Nine short flashes.

It couldn't make long ones.

I couldn't flash S-O-S.

This island would be my prison forever, and my evil jailer would return.

I dropped the net, held my face in my hands and sobbed.

"Good evening, Emily, I'm just taking Cadbury for his evening walk. You're out late, without a coat on. Is everything all right? Why are you standing outside Marine Rescue?"

"Hi, Oscar. Hi, Cadbury. I was looking for Shiraz. She told me she was meeting Anthony Blakey here to collect a document, but she hasn't come home again."

"That's right. I couldn't meet him myself, as I was at a council meeting. But she was supposed to see him two hours ago."

"She said she'd only be ten minutes. I'm worried. I received a call from her earlier, but she hung up."

"I'm sure she'll be fine, Emily. She probably pocket-dialled you. Maybe they decided to go for a drink together? He seemed, um, quite attracted to her. They probably went to the Smuggler's Tavern to escape that storm."

"That must be what's happened. I've been stood up. We were going to spend the evening with a bottle of Champagne trying on clothes and testing new hairstyles. She clearly prefers the company of a handsome man. Who would've thought a pirate's descendant would turn up all these years later and help save Blakey's Island?"

"I know. Look at it out there, silhouetted against the moonlight. It's a special place, and it doesn't need desecrating with a hotel."

"That's odd. Oscar, look. The cardinal mark's malfunctioned. It's supposed to flash nine times, isn't it?"

"Correct. West cardinal mark. But you're right. It's flashing some kind of random pattern. It must have a fault."

"It could almost be Morse code. We learnt that at Murph's training. He said we wouldn't use it these days, and I can't remember all the letters."

"I can. From my days as a marine rescue skipper. Three shorts. 'S'. Then four shorts. That's 'H'. Then two shorts. Which is 'I'. S-H-I. Now it's flashing S again. And H again, and I. Why on earth would it be doing that?"

"Oscar, it's Shiraz! S-H-I. The first three letters of her name. How on earth? What's she doing on the island? Oh, my goodness, she's signalling for help. We have to fetch her. I'll call Murph. This is an emergency."

The cardinal mark flashed three times, then I held the net to block its beam. I let it flash four times, then blocked it again, and let it shine the final two flashes. My arms ached, and I had no idea whether anyone had seen my signal, or even knew what it meant, but all I could do, over and over, was repeat S-H-I and think to myself how lucky I was that the first three letters of my name were entirely dots in Morse code.

I desperately wanted to stop and rest, but disrupting the light was all I could do to attract help. Exactly the same as the original pirate Thomas Blakey, all those years ago. Disrupting the light to attract ships. Except his intention was to wreck them. Mine was precisely the opposite.

I wondered who'd come. One of the commercial fishing boats, out at night? I couldn't remember what the tides were doing today, and whether the fleet would be at sea. The tourist boats wouldn't rescue me. Jim Turner and his competitors would be at home, watching TV, or in the Smugglers Tavern, enjoying a drink. They wouldn't be staring out to sea at Blakey's Island.

Maybe the hotel developers' yacht would cruise past? Why would they be out at night, though, in these waters?

Maybe the next boat to reach Blakey's Island would be my kidnapper, tomorrow morning?

I lowered the net and allowed the cardinal mark to continue its constant, uninterrupted sequence of nine flashes. My arms overflowed with pins and needles from being held constantly aloft.

No one was coming.

I was alone, abducted and abandoned.

"Hello, Murph speaking."

"Murph, it's Emily. I need your help. Shiraz is stuck on Blakey's Island."

"What d'you mean, Shiraz is on Blakey's Island? How did she get there? Nobody's allowed to land."

"I know she is, Murph. We have to launch the rescue vessel."

"Have you been drinking, Emily? Your words sounds slurred."

"I've had one or two Champagnes, yes. But we must help her. The west cardinal mark was flashing three dots, four dots, then two dots, over and over. S-H-I. The first three letters of Shiraz. Like we practised in training. It's her; she's definitely trapped on the island."

"Don't be ridiculous. How would she have got there, and how would she alter the flashes of the cardinal mark? She's not an electrician. The light must be faulty. Marine Rescue doesn't do navigation mark repairs. You'll need to report it to the maritime authorities."

"Please, look out of your window at Blakey's Island west cardinal mark at least? Tell me what you see."

"Faltering Fathometers. I'm in the middle of my favourite program, *Saving Lives at Sea*. All right. I'm looking out of my window at Blakey's Island. I can see the cardinal mark flashing nine times. As it's supposed to. And another nine. It seems to be working perfectly. Goodnight, Emily."

I rubbed my arms as the moon set, and its comforting, yellow glow over Blakey's Island beach turned terracotta-y orange as it flirted with the horizon.

No one would save me.

No commercial fishing vessels, no yachts, no rowing boats. I'd even have welcomed Anthony Blakey.

Frozen.

I'd no idea how long I'd been sitting on this rock, or, more urgently, how long I'd be here.

Should I return to the hut and await my fate? At least I'd be warmer, and I had the knife if Anthony returned. Although what would he return with? A gun? I gazed out again at the lights of Redcliff. I thought of Murph and his crew, who could save me so easily if only they knew my predicament. Was Emily still drinking Champagne and dancing in front of her mirror, singing into her hairbrush? I'd give anything to be with her.

Her bedroom light had gone out. She must've given up waiting for me and gone to sleep.

Hang on. It came on again.

And off.

And on.

Dash-dot-dot-dot.

Pause.

Three dashes, a pause, then another three dashes.

B-O-O.

I jumped up and grabbed the net as her bedroom light completed the sequence. A single dash, then three dots.

B-O-O-T-S.

She'd seen me.

Help was coming.

I let the cardinal mark flash three times, then my coat on a pole obscured the next flashes. I let it flash four times, then blocked the beam, followed by the final two flashes.

S-H-I.

My eyes strained across the water for the light of a vessel.

How long would it be?

Was that a red and a green? And which way around would they be if the boat was approaching me head on?

Green on the left, red on the right.

Rescue was coming from Redcliff Harbour.

And I was certain I knew who it'd be at the wheel.

"Stimulating scuttlebutts, Shiraz. What in heaven's name are you doing all the way out here by yourself?" Murph's voice yelled from the helm.

The Redcliff Marine Rescue vessel anchored in the shallows off Blakey's Island beach, and a crew member I recognised helped me aboard.

"It's rare we rescue one of our own," she said. "I'm Frances. I remember you from first aid training. Are you injured?"

"Cold, and wet below the knees. I'm sorry, this is becoming a habit. Please, I want to go home. I've had a terrible experience."

"So have I," said Murph. "I missed the end of my program, thanks to your capers. And my dinner will be cold."

"Gosh," said Frances. "Blakey's Island. I've always wanted to land here and see the puffins. It's a shame it's dark."

Murph started the engines and pulled up the anchor. "Whatever this was about, Shiraz, you're one lucky woman that Emily spotted your signal. I thought she was drunk. D'you know what she did? She rang the Coastguard and told them to page Redcliff Marine Rescue. She said it was a mayday, and her friend was stuck on Blakey's Island. Never in my ten years as a member of Marine Rescue has any crewman or woman summoned the boat by asking Coastguard to set off the pagers." He paused, as he swung the wheel, and we began the journey to Redcliff Harbour. "What the blazes were you doing here?"

"You'd never believe me if I told you. Please, take me home. I'm frozen. I promise I'll make this up to you."

I pressed my palms to my eyes and sobbed in relief as Frances wrapped a thick blanket around me and handed me a cup of warm water to sip from. I owed Emily dinner, a night out and several bottles of Champagne. Honestly, I owed her my life.

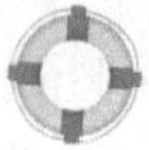

Emily waited on the harbour wall as Frances tied up the rescue boat. She threw her arms around me.

"I knew you were out there. I knew it. No one believed me. But what were you doing? And how did you get there?" She turned to Frances. "Thank you so much. I'll take care of her."

Murph looked at Emily and frowned. "Emily."

"Yes?"

He shook his head once. "I'm sure both of you are going to tell me later what this was about, but for now, keep warm and dry."

"Is that some kind of apology?"

"Apology?"

"For not believing me the first time."

"Maybe." Murph grumbled into his beard.

Emily gave him a hard stare, unlocked the door to our flat, and we clumped up the stairs.

"Hot drink, slip into your pyjamas and tell me what on earth happened tonight?" she said.

I faced her. "Nothing so relaxing. I'll change out of my wet boots and jeans, then we need to go to the police. Could you call Oscar and ask him to meet us? Safety in numbers."

"Now? At nine o'clock at night?"

"Yep. I'll explain on the way."

CHAPTER TWENTY-EIGHT

"You're in luck," said Oscar, as he pushed the police station door. "They're open. At some point in the evening, they shut Redcliff police and people have to ring the Headland Bay number."

A police officer who looked young enough to be at school stood behind the desk. "Evening. We're about to close. Is this an emergency?" His badge advertised him as PC Lachlan Davies.

"Yes," I said, placing both hands on the counter. "I wish to report an abduction. A kidnapping."

"Really?" he said, stiffening his posture. He flipped an iPad cover open and unclipped a stylus. "And who's been abducted?"

"Me. Shiraz Jones."

He frowned and pulled his head back. "Um, you've escaped, though?"

"Correct." Constable Lachlan must've been asleep during the how-to-deal-with-a-kidnapping lesson at police school.

"And who abducted you?"

"The same person who murdered Graham Woodhatch."

Constable Lachlan faced his palms towards me. "One thing at a time. Do you know the name of your, er, kidnapper?"

"Blakey."

He laid down his stylus and narrowed his eyes. "The pirate? He's been dead two hundred years."

"This is another Blakey, Anthony Blakey, a descendant of the pirate, who, when I last saw him, was very much alive. He arranged to meet me tonight to hand over a document."

Constable Lachlan scribbled on the iPad. "What kind of document?"

Oscar cleared his throat. "A legal document, connected with the council. This is all my fault; I should never have suggested Shiraz meet him alone, but he seemed so genuine."

"Seemed so genuine?" asked Lachlan. "You've met him before?"

"Twice, once in the Smuggler's Tavern and once at the Rotary Hall. We were discussing how he was going to help us with resisting this proposed hotel development."

"And, Ms Jones, where did you meet him when he, um, abducted you?"

"On the harbour wall by Redcliff Marine Rescue's building. He threatened me with a knife and told me to climb into his boat. He took me to Blakey's Island, and Marine Rescue saved me two hours later."

"He kidnapped you for two hours?"

"Constable," interrupted Oscar. "Have you ever interviewed the victim of a kidnapping? I was the Redcliff policeman for thirty years, and I never have. But I would imagine around now you'd be asking for a description of the suspect and alerting all police in the area. And maybe advise the sergeant? And victim support. This is a serious crime."

"I don't need victim support." I brushed his suggestion off and smiled. "Not when I have Emily's support."

Lachlan stood tall and leant over the desk. "I've done my training, sir. I am qualified to conduct this interview. Ms Jones, could you describe Blakey? Do you have a photo of him?"

"I don't. He's the same height as me when I'm not wearing heels. He presents as a smartly dressed city gentleman, with a closely cropped beard. Quite handsome, though I'm loathed to say that."

"Hair colour?"

"Dark. Almost black."

"Eye colour?"

"Brown."

"Do you have any contact details for him? An address, or a phone number?"

"His number's on a business card," said Oscar, "but it doesn't seem to work. He always calls me. Shiraz, he gave you his details, didn't he?"

"My phone's at the bottom of the sea, courtesy of Mr Blakey. We don't have his number, and we don't have an address. I think he's booked into a bed-and-breakfast."

Lachlan rubbed his chin. "We could call around the hotels and guest houses and discover if anyone fitting that description's staying, or was staying. Unfortunately, all our resources are taken up investigating this fisherman's murder; I'll have to contact the sergeant and see who we can spare."

"See who you can spare?" blustered Oscar. "We're dealing with a kidnapping, not a parking ticket."

"Thank you, sir. I'm well aware of the severity of the crime." Lachlan swiped up on the iPad. "Ms Jones, what makes you think he, um, murdered Graham Woodhatch?"

"Because Marine Rescue found Graham's boat adrift off Blakey's Island. And when Anthony Blakey took me to the island, I discovered sets of clothes which looked too big for him. I think they might've belonged to Graham."

"That's a leap of imagination. They could be anybody's. Did you discover items with Mr Woodhatch's name on them, which might prove your theory more conclusively?"

"No. I didn't want to touch anything. Oh, and something else. Graham's boat had no fishing gear on board when

Marine Rescue found it, despite him being a keen angler. I discovered a collection of rods and tackle boxes on the island. They might be his too."

"They might be, but we don't know that, and it's an even bigger stretch of imagination to say that because fishing gear found on Blakey's Island may have belonged to Mr Woodhatch, this Anthony Blakey murdered him. Regardless, I'll add it to the case notes."

I shrugged. What else could I tell him? "At least you'll look for Anthony Blakey? He's definitely a kidnapper, even if he's not a murderer."

"Yep. We'll get on to that immediately. I'll contact Sergeant Will and the duty sergeant at Headland Bay Police. Rest assured we'll mobilise all our assets immediately."

"Hmph," said Oscar, under his breath. "That sounds like a line straight from a TV cop programme."

Constable Lachlan glared at him. "I think I have everything I need. Apart from your contact details. We'll need to interview you again about this, I'm sure."

I explained I lived with Emily, and we gave her phone number to call me until I replaced my phone. Oscar left his information too.

"I'm not going to sleep now, after that experience," I said, as we returned to Emily's apartment through Redcliff's quiet streets. I continually glanced left, right and over my shoulder, expecting Anthony Blakey to jump out of the shadows at any moment.

"Me neither," said Emily. "I'll text Angela and ask her to open the café first thing. She seems very capable and loves the work. Oscar, would you walk home with us? I know it's late, but there's a kidnapper on the loose."

"And a murderer," I said. "I'm convinced Anthony Blakey murdered Graham Woodhatch. Once we're upstairs, I'll explain their connection."

CHAPTER TWENTY-NINE

Anthony Blakey stared out to sea from his accommodation window and held his head in his hands.

Everything had gone wrong.

Everything.

He'd watched the lights of the rescue boat leave the harbour and had a terrible, sinking feeling he knew where it headed. Every minute it sped away from Redcliff, he prayed it would veer off and zoom along the coast, but he tracked its dead-straight path to Blakey's Island.

His island.

Somehow, his fiancée had summoned them.

How dare she? He had such wonderful plans for their lives together. How could she be so ungrateful? After all he'd done to prepare their new home.

How could she choose a life without him, over a life with him at her side? It made no sense.

Why hadn't she realised he was handing her a perfect paradise on a plate?

And now she'd have told them the story, and they'd be searching for him.

He needed to grab his possessions and make his escape.

Lie low, until this had all been forgotten, and he could devise another plan to force her to see sense.

One thing nagged at his mind as he stuffed his gentleman-about-town clothes into his suitcase.

While she was sitting on the beach, waiting for him, her lover, to return, had she discovered the real secret of Blakey's Island?

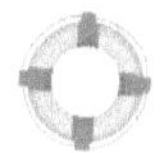

CHAPTER THIRTY

Emily double-locked the front door behind us as we climbed the stairs. She also slid the safety chain across, something I'd never seen her do before.

"What an evening," said Oscar, removing his coat.

"Glass of wine?" asked Emily. "Or something stronger?"

"Much as I enjoy a single malt, wine would be most welcome. I think we all need something to steady our nerves. Especially you, Shiraz, after what you've been through."

"Yes," I said. "Sorry, Emily, we never finished our dress-ups."

"Goodness, don't apologise." She glugged a bottle of dark, blackcurranty Cabernet Sauvignon into three glasses. "There's plenty of time for that. We need to make sure you're okay first. I won't be able to sleep until Blakey's caught."

"Me neither. I hope they track him down quickly. The entire experience has left me shaking."

"If you feel able to, talk us through it again," said Oscar. "The quick chat we had on the way to the police station didn't answer all my questions. I need to write things down. Emily, pass the pad and pen, please."

I took multiple sips of wine in an attempt to stop the trembling as I relived the evening's events. "Anthony Blakey met me as arranged. I asked him for the document he'd promised, proving his claim. He told me he'd secreted it on the island, and he'd take me there to collect it. I became suspicious."

"Of course," said Emily. She rubbed my back. "You poor thing."

"Unfortunately, not suspicious enough. I should've run away immediately." My teeth bit my lip. "I wish I had. Although, then we'd never have known what he was up to."

"And what was he up to, exactly?" asked Oscar.

"I told him to fetch the document; I wouldn't come with him. At that point he became threatening and pulled me towards his boat. That was the one, Emily, we saw on the island during night training. With 'Ruth' on the stern. He must've been chugging back and forth regularly."

"He must. Gosh, you drank that quickly," said Emily, noticing my empty glass and topping it up.

"Then, he twisted my arm behind my back and held a knife to my throat. I screamed for you, but your music was turned up so high you couldn't hear me."

She stood and threw her arms around me. "Here's me, dancing in front of the mirror and singing into my hairbrush, and not fifty metres away you're being assaulted. Shiraz, I'm so sorry."

"Goodness, Emily, I'm not blaming you. None of us would ever have thought this could happen."

"No," said Oscar, clenching his teeth. "He seemed so genuine, so professional."

"Anyway, the strangest thing was, he started calling me 'darling', like I was his girlfriend. He told me he'd take me to his island, where we'd live happily for the rest of our lives."

"Urgh." Emily shuddered. "What a creep."

"To think I'd found him attractive when I first met him. He said he'd always wanted me, and he couldn't live without me."

"Stop," said Oscar, holding up his pencil and pointing it at me. "There's something missing here. D'you think Anthony Blakey's desires towards you had sprung up since you first met in the Smuggler's Tavern last weekend? Because his language suggests he'd been planning this a long time."

I wrinkled my lips. "I wondered if I'd seen Blakey before. But then I decided I must've known someone who looked like him, or maybe he has a generic face."

Oscar rubbed his chin. "Hmm. Let's come back to that."

"Something in a retired police officer's training which raised your hackles?" asked Emily.

"Definitely," said Oscar. "There's more to this story than a desire to stop a hotel development and a claim to the island. Possibly more than a kidnapping. I think all these matters connect. But carry on, Shiraz."

I drank more wine. "We began the boat journey to Blakey's Island. He held the knife against me the whole time and kept telling me we were going to start our new lives together there."

"So creepy," said Emily. She puffed out her cheeks.

"I racked my brains to think of ways to escape him or overpower him. Something came to me which I'd read in a novel about kidnapping, where a private investigator said, the longer someone's captive, the less likely they are to escape. So I knew my actions had to be quick. As the boat beached on the island, he slipped, and I took my chance. I whipped my phone out of my pocket and pressed the first button I could, which was redial. The last number I'd called was yours, Emily, but, as you answered, Anthony snatched the phone from me and threw it into the sea."

"Oh, no. I thought you must've pocket dialled me. How things would've been different if we'd connected."

"Yes. Unfortunately, we didn't. Then he marched me into the old warden's hut and told me that'd be our new marital home."

"Marital?" exclaimed Emily. "He thought you were his wife? He's deluded."

"He said he was going to fetch food and a whole new wardrobe of clothes for me in his favourite colours, including red shoes. Which is strange, as he's never seen me in red shoes. I didn't bring any with me when I moved from London."

"That proves it," said Oscar. "You must've been acquainted with him in the past. Are you sure he's not a jilted ex from long ago, or someone you'd declined in your city life?"

I forced a laugh. "I was married for nearly twenty years. And unlike my erstwhile husband, I could stay faithful. It's true I had my admirers; which society girl doesn't? But I've certainly had no relationships on the side. Compared to many ladies with my background, I'm innocent."

Oscar squirmed in his seat. "Sorry, Shiraz. I wasn't intimating anything. But I'm certain Anthony Blakey knew you before. That, I think, is the key to this whole mystery. What happened next?"

I elbowed him, and he dropped the knife. It fell on the floor, and I was able to grab it. Hah! That rattled him. He ran back to his boat and motored away, shouting I didn't realise who I was dealing with, and he'd be back. He said there was no way I could escape."

I finished my second glass of wine and held my flat hand over it to show Emily I didn't want any more. Which wasn't true. I could've drunk the entire bottle and then another one, but that wouldn't help solve this enigma.

"Hmph," said Oscar. "Thanks to your Morse code training, his statement was wrong, thank goodness."

"Then what did you do?" asked Emily.

"I wasn't going to sit in the hut and cry."

"Of course you weren't," she said, putting her arm around me. "The Shiraz I know's made of tougher stuff."

"Yep. I wondered if I could swim, so I tested the sea to discover how cold it was."

"Freezing," said Oscar. "It's a good job you didn't try. You would've died from cold, or drowning, or both."

"Then, by the water, I found Anthony's torch, which he must've dropped. I flashed S-O-S at the mainland, but the beam was too weak to shine far. I searched the island for something else to help me. That's when I found those clothes in the hut, and the fishing gear. And I think they're Graham Woodhatch's. I never met Graham, but, Oscar, you said he was a sturdy chap?"

"Yes; he wasn't the fittest person."

"I remember," said Emily. "He enjoyed my chocolate pastries, and often bought two. I knew they were both for him."

"These clothes were too big for Anthony," I continued. "And I remember you told me Graham was a smoker? I think Angela said that too."

"Yep. He often attended council meetings with a pipe sticking out of the corner of his mouth, unlit, of course. Did you find a pipe?"

"No, but the room smelt of pipe smoke. Like someone had recently been smoking there. My granddad smoked a pipe, and the smell reminded me of him. Then, I explored around the rear of the hut, and I found the fishing gear. It must be Graham's. His boat was discovered off the beach. We noticed it had no equipment in it, and there are all these rods and tackle boxes on the island where no-one's supposed to land."

"Got it," said Emily. "Anthony Blakey was living on the island, up to no good. Graham was fishing nearby and happened to see him there. In order to prevent detection, Anthony motored out to Graham's boat in his tender, killed him, carved a 'B' in his chest as a nod to his pirate descendant, threw him overboard, stole his fishing gear and smoky-smelling clothes, and took them back to the island. Case closed." She thumped the table and gave a triumphant grin.

I laughed for the first time since my abduction. "Congratulations, Emily. This time, I think you're right."

Oscar finished scribbling, laid down his pencil and looked up. "Your theory sounds plausible. There's a loose end, though, that we've all overlooked. How does any of this tie in with the proposed hotel development, and Anthony Blakey's meetings with us?"

"Easy," said Emily. "Anthony Blakey didn't want the hotel development to go ahead, because he needed to keep Blakey's Island as Shiraz's boudoir."

"Boudoir." I snorted. "I haven't heard that word for, like, ever. But I see what you mean. And maybe he killed Graham and carved that 'B' in his chest to frighten the developers off. To make them think it wouldn't be worth building a hotel on the island because the pirate story was still relevant today, and pirates were still boarding boats and murdering captains."

"Dear me," said Oscar, shaking his head. "Now we are off into the realms of fantasy."

"But Shiraz might be right," said Emily. "Anthony Blakey clearly has a screw loose, kidnapping Shiraz and convincing himself she'll happily live with him as his wife on the island. Maybe he killed Graham for that reason?"

"All unknowns," said Oscar. "Guesswork. I still think the hotel developers had a hand in the murder." He looked at his watch. "Goodness, it's almost midnight. I really must go home. You ladies will be safe shut up in here. Keep the doors and windows locked."

"We will, don't worry." Emily stood and collected the empty glasses. "Oh, before you leave, Oscar, what was the outcome of the council meeting?"

"Gosh, yes, that seems days ago, but it was only this evening. A lot's happened since then."

I puffed. "Tell me about it."

"The councillors brushed over the real crux of the discussion, which should've been the negative impact this development might have on Redcliff, and instead talked about how much they'd enjoyed the yacht trip, the wine and the food. Bribery, that's what it was, pure bribery. My involuntary ducking was the subject of much mirth. And, seeing as the police say there's no evidence for my story of being pushed, I could hardly keep bringing it up. Nobody seemed to care Graham wasn't present; it's like he's forgotten, and the rest of the members are jostling for the position of deputy mayor. They're parasites, the lot of them. Anyway, the vote passed to proceed to the next stage. I wonder at what point the plans I saw on the yacht will come to light? The proper plans. Probably not until construction starts. Then those idiots will know what they've really voted for. Thanks for the wine. I'll see myself out."

Emily swiped her keys from the table. "I'll be right behind you to lock the door."

As Oscar walked down the stairs, Emily's phone rang, and she disturbed Boots' sleep to grab it off the couch. "Hello? Yes, she's here." She held up her palm to instruct Oscar not to leave yet and handed the phone to me. "Police," she mouthed.

"Hi, this is Shiraz Jones. Really? That was quick. Where was he? Yes, certainly we'll come. Tomorrow morning at ten? See you then. And thank you, Sergeant. This is a weight off my shoulders. I've spent the whole evening shaking. Goodbye."

I handed the phone back to Emily. "That was Sergeant Will. They arrested Anthony Blakey this evening at Redcliff Railway Station, about to board the night train to the city."

CHAPTER THIRTY-ONE

"They arrested your kidnapper?" Emily pressed a palm to her heart. "Thank goodness for that. Now we don't need to feel like prisoners in our home, with the doors and windows shuttered and barred."

"I take back my opinion of Constable Lachlan," said Oscar. "He did us proud; we only reported this incident three hours ago. I imagined you'd have to go through further interviews, helping the police construct lookalike photos, and all the time in fear for your life."

"I do have to attend an identity parade tomorrow morning. They'd like you there too, if possible, Oscar. Emily, you're excused. You might have trouble identifying Blakey. As soon as you saw him, you, um, fell flat on the pub floor."

"Thank you. You don't need to remind me. Very embarrassing."

"I can be there at ten tomorrow," said Oscar. "Or should I say, today? It's one minute past midnight. Goodnight, ladies."

He clumped down to the front door and slammed it shut behind him.

Emily yawned and stretched. "Bedtime. And a lie-in tomorrow. Angela said she'd open the café. I'll get up when you do."

I laughed. "9:30? Four hours after your normal waking time."

"Perfect. It's been a massive day for both of us."

Daffodils poked through earth in tubs outside Redcliff's front doors, and white clouds drifted in a northerly breeze across a pale-blue sky as Oscar and I entered the police station once more.

"Good morning, Ms Jones." Sergeant Will Bishopstone shook my hand and nodded at Oscar. "Thank you both for attending today. This has been quite an event, hasn't it?"

"Um, yes. I've never been kidnapped before."

"Few people have, thank goodness. Come into the interview room, and I'll bring you up to speed before the identity parade." He led us into the stark, cell-like office with four chairs, and we sat opposite him, the Formica table between us.

Oscar smiled at the sergeant. "Congratulations on a job well done. How did you catch him so quickly? You didn't have a photo or much to go on, beyond our description."

"We'd begun to knock on doors of accommodation providers in the town, starting with the small hotels and guest houses. We would've moved down the list to the bed-and-breakfasts and Air B'n'Bs, had we no luck there. The owners didn't appreciate being disturbed at that time in the evening, but speed was of the essence in case he was planning an escape."

"Which, by the sound of it, he was."

"Indeed. We heard a report from the dispatcher about an incident at Redcliff Railway Station. I made no connection and sent a car to drive past. It seems our Mr Blakey attempted to board the night train, which carries goods, milk and other produce from Redcliff destined for tomorrow morning's city markets. There's only one carriage for passengers. All was in order with Mr Blakey's ticket, but the train guard took exception to the large packing case on wheels accompanying him. There was no room in the passenger car for it, and he hadn't pre-booked space in the goods section. Mr Blakey shoved the guard to the ground and attempted to drag the large box into the carriage. By a stroke of luck, three members of Redcliff Rugby Club happened to be on the same train, heading for London to watch the international match tomorrow. They saw the commotion, overpowered Blakey, and sat on him until the police arrived. If you're trying to make a quick exit, the last thing you want is three rugby players using you as a couch. And when our car reached the station, we realised this was the man we were all searching for."

"How?" I asked. "From my description?"

"Yes, but also, he'd helpfully stencilled 'A Blakey' on the side of his packing case."

We all laughed.

"If only every criminal was so amenable," said Oscar.

"Indeed," said Sergeant Will. "Let's do the identity parade now, then you can leave."

Oscar and I strolled along the seafront towards the café and home.

"I'll bet you're glad all that's over with," he said. "The sergeant told me they'd be questioning him about Graham's murder too. I was so sure the developers were involved in that somehow, but your discovery of what appear to be Graham's possessions on the island is fairly conclusive. Hopefully, Blakey confesses. Shall I buy you a coffee?"

"Thank you. I've only had one today."

He held open the door of the Wicked Whelk, and Angela greeted us from behind the counter. "Good morning, Shiraz. Good morning, Oscar. Double shot, skinny latte and black Earl Grey tea?"

"Yes, please." I said. "Where's Emily?"

"I'm here," said a voice behind us. "Thanks so much, Angela. I could never have opened at six after last night."

"Oh?" Angela frowned. "What happened last night?"

Oscar glanced daggers at Emily, and I remembered the location of Graham's death. Probably best not to talk about Blakey's Island.

"I was, um, unexpectedly detained," she said. "All okay now, though. Er, isn't it a beautiful, spring day?"

"Yes," said Angela. "Graham said this looked like a perfect day for fishing."

"I'm sorry," said Oscar, "Graham said?"

"Um, Graham would've said." Angela covered her mouth. "I still can't believe he's gone."

"Of course," said Emily. "Do you want to knock off now? I can take over. Thanks so much for managing the morning rush."

"My pleasure. I'll go home and put my feet up. See you tomorrow."

"Goodness, tomorrow's Saturday already. We'll be busy with family breakfasts, so I'm glad there'll be two of us. Bye, Angela."

"Poor woman," said Oscar, after she'd left. "She still speaks about her husband as if he's alive."

"Yes," I said. "She told me she keeps thinking he's going to walk back in the door. Anyway, what are your plans for this afternoon?"

"Digging the vegetable garden, preparing to plant spring seeds. You?"

Emily placed our drinks in front of us. "This afternoon, Shiraz and I are revising from our marine rescue workbooks."

"We are?" I shrugged and frowned.

"Yep. We're out on the boat tomorrow. And I'll bet Murph tests us about lights and cardinal marks."

"If he asks us about Morse code, I'll answer correctly. I'm probably the only one of us who's used it for real."

"Indeed," said Oscar. "What a good job you'd learnt enough of it."

"And, in the evening," said Emily, "could we do what we planned last night, before your, um, experience? Try on some outfits and different hair styles? I'm waiting to hear back from David; I think I have a date tomorrow."

"Wow. Congratulations. Of course we can. Where's he taking you?"

"We're meeting at the Smuggler's Tavern. They have a band on Saturday evenings. I hope you can lend me dancing shoes."

"I'll leave you to it," said Oscar. "My wife wants to go shopping in Headland Bay, and for once, I'd like to accompany her. I need to find a new phone. People keep ringing the home phone complaining they can't contact me."

"Which one are you buying?" I asked.

"I've no idea. My son's meeting me at the phone shop and helping me choose."

"While you're there, could you see how much the new model iPhone is? I'm going to purchase it next time I visit Headland Bay."

Emily stood in front of her mirror, wearing my brown Gucci wedges which we'd thankfully retrieved from the Smuggler's Tavern, my shimmering, silver dress which she'd pinned up to suit her height and a thin, white belt she'd bought. We'd scattered a selection of discarded clothes on her bed. "Le Freak," by Chic blared from speakers, and she twisted and jiggled to the beat.

"This doesn't work," she said. "It's the right length on you, but it looks stupid below my knees."

"We can't pin it up any higher," I yelled, as the disco segued into "Go West," by Village People. "We could cut it and run it through your sewing machine."

"But then you wouldn't be able to wear it anymore."

"I have lots of dresses. You can have it. A present for giving me free accommodation. I'm not exactly pulling my weight in the café."

"Hmm." Emily pretended to look stern. "You'll need to give me a dress every week, then." She laughed, and I joined in.

THUMP THUMP THUMP

"Police knock," I said. "That must be Oscar."

"What's he doing here? Could you answer it while I change?"

THUMP THUMP THUMP

"All right, I'm coming." I nipped down the stairs.

"Hi, Oscar. What brings you here?"

"Hello, Shiraz. Sorry to disturb your man-free evening, but I have news you two will want to hear."

Oh? You'd better come in."

"Where's Emily?" he asked, at the top of the stairs.

"I'm changing," yelled Emily from the bedroom. "Take a seat. I'll be there in a minute."

I cleared a newspaper off the sofa, and Boots objected as I shifted him onto the floor. We sat, then Oscar stood when Emily entered.

"I didn't think this could wait," he said. "There's news about Anthony Blakey's arrest."

"Oh?" Emily and I said together.

"Yes. While Anthony Blakey's clearly guilty of kidnap, they've concluded he's innocent of Graham's murder."

"Seriously?" I said. "I was convinced of his guilt."

Oscar pulled a pad from his pocket and referred to it. "The police have interviewed Blakey. They were trying to call you, Emily, to speak with Shiraz, but you weren't answering, so they rang my home number. I can't wait until I pick up my new mobile tomorrow. Sometimes I daren't leave the house while waiting for important calls."

"We may've had the music too loud," I said, sharing a grin with Emily. "Sorry they disturbed you."

"It's a good job they did. You know me, I let nothing get past my nose, and I enjoy finding information which, um, may not be available through regular channels. I popped up to the police station and discovered some details." He lowered his voice. "Are you ready for this?"

We both nodded and sat forward in our seats.

Oscar took a deep breath. "Anthony Blakey isn't his real name."

"I knew it," said Emily. "The pirate connection was too coincidental."

"But he showed us his driving licence," I said. "We both saw 'Anthony Blakey' on that."

"Correct. I should rephrase my statement. His legal name is Anthony Blakey. Five weeks ago, he changed it by deed poll. Formerly, he was known as Bozidar Radic."

My hand flew to my mouth. "Bozidar Radic? I hoped I'd never hear that name again in my life."

CHAPTER THIRTY-TWO

"So you know this Bozidar Radic?" asked Oscar. "I was sure he'd seen you before, from his intimations about outfits you wore."

"I know *of* him." I shuddered. "He was arrested for stalking me last year. The police found him in my garden with a long-lens camera. They told me he possessed photos he'd taken of me. Thousands of them, displayed on his living room wall. He'd attended every public event I'd been at: movie premieres, nightclub celebrations, society parties, and he'd taken secret photos at each one. Not only that"—I felt my skin crawl—"he'd snapped me while shopping, at the gym, on my husband's yacht and even in my underwear through my bedroom window. He had pictures of me dating back five years. I can't believe I've been face-to-face with him. In the same room. On the same island. Alone. Gosh. My insides are churning thinking about it."

Oscar flipped his pad over to the next page. "He was imprisoned for nine months on the stalking charge and released eight weeks ago. Conditions of his discharge were that he never went within one hundred metres of you, he never tried to photograph you, he wasn't allowed to possess any images of you and couldn't own a high-powered camera."

"Fair enough. Clearly, he hasn't got over his obsession."

"Correct. As soon as he was released, he set out to track you down again, but you'd vanished. Of course, you'd left your husband and made a new life down here, but he wasn't to know that, until he saw your picture alongside Murph and Emily in a newspaper article about marine rescue. That alerted him to your move to Redcliff."

"Gosh, I remember that photo being taken. I wish I hadn't let them print it now."

"A natural reaction," said Oscar. "Anyway, he hatched an elaborate plot to follow you here and kidnap you. We'll never know the details, but what we do know is that Bozidar Radic legally changed his name to Anthony Blakey as part of his plot and then approached me, through the council, to sell us his fairy story about being a descendant of the pirate. His warped plan involved claiming ownership of the island, turning the old warden's hut into a prison and whisking you away to live there. He must've jumped for joy inside when I introduced you to each other at the Smuggler's Tavern. I'm sorry I ever did."

"How could you have known?" I said. "He was very persuasive. Beguiling, even. To think I almost fell for him, found him attractive." I paused. "You mentioned, when you arrived, that he couldn't have murdered Graham. What makes you so sure? He seems capable of anything."

"I know he didn't murder Graham. The night of Graham's death, Bozidar Radic was in police custody."

"I thought you said he'd been released?"

"He had. Remember, one condition of his bail was that he couldn't own a high-powered camera. During a traffic stop, the police found him with a long-lensed Nikon on his passenger seat, they arrested him, and he spent the night in cells. The same night, Graham went missing."

"Why did they let him go? Surely they should've sent him back to prison for breaking the terms of his parole."

"He must've employed a talented lawyer, as he successfully argued the camera wasn't his. Regardless, he couldn't have had a better alibi."

"Back to square one," said Emily. "I knew it was those developers. Johnny Chadwick and his cronies. They tried to kill you, Oscar. They must've killed Graham."

"They certainly would seem to be the most obvious suspects," said Oscar. "At least we've ruled one person from our list. Anthony Blakey, AKA Bozidar Radic, was not responsible for Graham's murder."

Saturday morning.

Seabirds crying.

Children's shouts.

A dog's bark.

The assorted noises outside woke me in the middle of a dream. One of those horrible dreams which seems so real on waking. Everyone has them, right? In the first few seconds of wakefulness, you one hundred per cent know what you just experienced in your nightmare really happened. And then, the gradual realisation it didn't and, in the real world, you've earnt a second chance.

A second chance to unsay the words you hadn't meant.

A second chance to undo the hurt you'd caused your most loved one by actions in your dream.

Or a second chance to decline a solo meeting with Anthony Blakey.

Otherwise known as Bozidar Radic.

In my dream, I stood in a garden, wearing a veil, a shimmering, silver dress and holding a flower garland. Oscar waited on my left, and Emily held the hem of my outfit. I turned, and behind me stretched an aisle of rose petals. White birds flew around the scene, and a beautifully dressed man of my height approached slowly. His neatly bearded face was indistinct, but I knew his name.

I'd known it for years.

He reached me, lifted the veil and leant in to kiss me.

I sat up in bed drenched in sweat, one hundred per cent sure I was about to marry Bozidar Radic.

Thank goodness for the second chance.

Now the police had charged him with kidnapping, hopefully he'd go to prison for years, and I'd never hear his name again. I tugged back the curtain and felt free. Free of his clutches. Free, in the knowledge he couldn't photograph me, abduct me or hurt me again.

Life would be normal now.

And the first normal action, on every normal day which I would normally do, was to buy a coffee.

My coffee requirements were anything but normal.

"Hi, Angela, Hi, Emily." I swung open the door of the Wicked Whelk.

"Goodness," said Angela. "This is early for you, isn't it? It's not even 9:30. The usual double shot, skinny latte?"

"In a take-away cup, please. A horrible dream woke me. And I don't want to go back to sleep in case it restarts."

"I know that feeling," said Emily. "The other morning, I dreamt David and I went on a restaurant date, and he ended up going home with the waitress."

"Who's David?" asked Angela. "Your boyfriend?"

Emily blushed. "Not yet. An acquaintance."

"Aww, young love," said Angela. "When Graham and I began courting, he was nineteen and I was seventeen."

"Gosh, that was young," I said. "Where was your first date?"

"The cinema." She laughed. "I know, very traditional."

"What did you see?"

"*Diamonds are Forever*. I thought it was a love story. Well, you would, wouldn't you, with the title? It was more his type of movie than mine. But I enjoyed it, and we've seen all the James Bond movies together since. We're looking forward to the next one."

"I'm sorry, did you say 'we'?"

"I mean, I'm looking forward to the next one. Pardon me. I can't get out of the habit of saying 'we' about everything."

Emily rubbed Angela's shoulder. "It must be so hard, suddenly losing your husband like that. Here's your coffee, Shiraz." She glared at me, and I inwardly chastised myself for my insensitivity. I was sure she couldn't have killed him.

"Thanks. I'll take a morning stroll. See you at boat training this afternoon."

Thoughts of what I'd said to Angela filled my mind as I strolled around the harbour wall, on what was rapidly becoming my regular morning take-away-coffee-sipping walk. That feeling when you've said something stupid and upset someone, and you keep replaying the conversation over and over and wishing you could turn back time? A lot of that was happening recently. I hadn't meant anything when I'd queried her use of the word 'we'; I genuinely wondered who she was talking about.

Assorted-shaped white clouds competed with grey ones in an overcast sky. Fishing boats, pleasure cruisers, little rowing skiffs and yachts bobbed up and down with the light swell, and commercial trawlers lay tied up along the harbour wall. I greeted Jim Turner, who responded with, "Ahoy there, me hearty lass," and I laughed.

My hand shielded my eyes as I scanned the boats for the open, wooden craft Bozidar Radic had forced me into at knifepoint. Several boats resembled it, but none had the name *Ruth* on the stern. Maybe the police had removed it? Sweat moistened my forehead as I recalled that evening— was it only two days ago?—and how they'd caught him so quickly.

But they hadn't caught Graham's killer.

We knew it wasn't suicide, or an accident. No one carves a letter in their own chest. I glanced down and traced a 'B' with my finger across my breastbone. Impossible. Probably not even achievable while looking in a full-length mirror.

We knew it wasn't Bozidar Radic. He had the best alibi of all.

It must've been Johnny Chadwick and the hotel developers. After all, they'd thrown Oscar off the yacht. If that wasn't attempted murder, what was? And then lied to the police to cover it up. So they were very capable of breaking the law. Ve-ery capable. Maybe the police were busy investigating them?

Could I help uncover some clues? I didn't think any police had been to Blakey's Island, following my discovery of the clothes and fishing gear. And those possessions would be a clue, right? Maybe the murderer left some fingerprints or DNA on the belongings. How would the police reach the island? They didn't have a boat. Would Marine Rescue give them a ride? Murph wouldn't like that. I laughed to myself as I imagined his reaction. "Ferry the police? Galloping galleons. We're not a taxi service."

I arrived early at boat training that afternoon and caught Murph enjoying a lie down on the couch.

"Afternoon, Murph. Sorry to disturb your siesta."

He opened one eye and frowned at me. "Siesta? I'm not having a siesta. I'd finished repairing the electrics on the boat, and this sofa needed testing." He glanced at the clock above the door. "You're early. Was there something in the marine rescue workbook you needed to ask me about?"

"Um, no. But I was hoping to ask you a favour. I need to return to Blakey's Island."

"You're a sucker for punishment, aren't you? Two days ago, we rescued you from what I've heard was some kind of abduction. I would've thought it'd be the last place you'd want to see again. I've told you, we can't just land there without good reason. It's out of bounds; you know that. Why do you want to see it again?"

"You remember how you found Graham Woodhatch's boat adrift? When I was on the island, I discovered possessions I thought might be his. But it was dark, and I'd like to inspect them again in the light."

"That's not a valid reason for us to land there. His death doesn't concern us, does it? We rescue living people; or sometimes help the Coastguard recover bodies. We don't investigate why people died. That's a job for the police."

His pocket vibrated as his mobile phone rang.

"Murph speaking. Hello, Terry. You're not going to ask me to escort another millionaire's gin palace, I hope? Good."

A pause, while the caller spoke in Murph's ear, and he grimaced.

"They want what? How many of them? Perishing Picaroons, we're not a taxi service."

I hid a grin with my hand.

"I see," continued Murph. "An official request. All right. But I'm the skipper, and they'll do as I say. They'll have to complete a safety induction, and if we get a rescue job, that'll take priority. They understand that, right? Fine. We'll see them at three. Bye, Terry."

Murph snapped his phone closed and turned to me. "Shiraz, you're getting your wish. Terry's asked us to transport two police officers to Blakey's Island. I don't know why, but I presume it's something to do with what you found there. Ah, hello, Emily. Hello, David. Welcome to Redcliff Chauffeur-driven Marine Limousines. Airports, weddings, offshore islands. No job too small."

CHAPTER THIRTY-THREE

Six people on board the marine rescue boat were two too many. Murph, David, Frances and me politely danced the dosey-do, bumping together as we manoeuvred around the cabin. The two police officers accompanying us were Sergeant Will Bishopstone, who I'd met before, and Detective Fay Walker from Headland Bay Police, who I hadn't. Neither looked comfortable sporting spare sets of marine rescue overalls. Fay was tall and thin, with short hair, and although she seemed friendly, I kept my guard up, as I suspected she was subtly interviewing me.

"This is an unexpected bonus," said Fay, "travelling with the marine rescue volunteer who discovered the clothes on the island. Have you been a member for long?"

"No," I said. "This is my second month."

"Enjoying it?"

"Loving it. It's so rewarding, rescuing people in trouble."

"I understand," said Fay, "you were rescued yourself two nights ago."

I sucked in a breath. "Yes. Someone, who I didn't want to go with, took me to the island."

"We're dealing with him as part of a separate investigation," said Sergeant Will. "Unrelated to this matter."

"Your town certainly has a lot of crime," said Fay to Will. "Not like Headland Bay. Hardly anything happens there."

I couldn't decipher whether she was having a dig at Will about how crime-ridden his beat was, or bemoaning she had nothing to do.

"Hold on to something," said Murph. "Coming down."

He slowed the boat, and we drifted gently to shore. I heard the scrunch of sand as we beached.

"Here's how this is going to work," he said. "The most important thing is safety. Hold on with both hands, climb down the ladder at the starboard side of the vessel, then wade through the shallow water. Use each other for support if necessary and watch your feet. There are small rocks you could trip over. Shiraz and Frances will accompany the police going ashore. David will remain with me on the boat. If we need to leave suddenly, I'll sound the horn like this."

He tooted twice, and we all jumped.

"That's a loud horn, Murph," said Will. "We'll hear it anywhere on the island."

"How long d'you think you'll be?"

"That's hard to tell," said Fay. "It depends on what we find. Hopefully, less than an hour."

"An hour?" exclaimed Murph. "I'll set the meter to waiting time."

Will turned to me. "Shiraz, could you please lead us to where you found the clothes and fishing gear?"

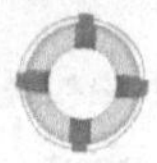

The smell hit me first. The smoky smell, which once transported me back to my grandfather's arms, but now reminded me of the night of my kidnapping. I shuddered.

"Are you all right, Ms Jones?" asked Detective Fay.

"No, not really. This brings back horrible memories. I've shown you the hut, and the fishing gear's behind it. Could you excuse me? I'll wait on the beach."

"Of course. We'll take it from here." The two police officers began searching for evidence, opening the furniture drawers.

"I can't believe I was marooned here only two nights ago," I said to Frances, as we stood on the beach in our bright-yellow waterproofs. "It looks so different in the light. I'm not sure I could return here after dark."

"I'm sure you won't have to," said Frances. "I suppose it depends on what happens with this hotel. You might return as a guest?"

I laughed. "My swanky hotel days are behind me."

"Look. Puffins." Frances pointed at little orange blobs dotting crevices in the rocks. "Let's take photos." She unzipped a pocket, pulled a phone out, raised it to her eyes and snapped several shots.

"Um, they're very distant," I said, as she showed me the pictures. "It's hard to tell they're birds."

"Shall we try to get closer?" she suggested. "There's a goat-track of a path to the right. If we climbed, we'd be level with their nests."

"We might frighten them, in our yellow overalls and boots."

"That can't be helped. We'll be as quiet as we can."

We shuffled up the beach and ducked into the bushes at the rear. The path Frances had spotted wasn't an official one made by humans; more a series of steps up the boulders. The smell of seabird increased as we ascended.

"Shh," she said, turning around to me. "This'll do." She zoomed her phone and photographed the birds. I glanced over my shoulder and gazed at the rescue boat, beached on the sand one hundred yards below us like a child's bath toy.

Murph leant out of the cabin, gesticulated at us, yelled and beckoned, so I tapped Frances on the shoulder. "I think we should go. Murph's not keen on us being up here. Look."

I pointed at the waving, bearded figure.

"He's spoiling our fun," said Frances. "Probably worried we'll slip."

The two police left the hut carrying clear, plastic bags with dark bundles inside them.

"It's time to depart," I said. "The police have finished."

We clambered down, pushed back through the bushes and met Will and Fay at the boat.

"Did you find what you were looking for?" I asked. "D'you know who the clothes belong to?"

"No," said Fay. "There's nothing conclusive. Although, it looks like the bed's been slept in."

"How can you tell that?" I imagined they'd have some technical, bed-testing equipment.

"A dent in the pillow. Did you lie on the bed on Thursday night?"

"Definitely not. Yuck."

"Maybe it was your abductor," said Will. "But the clothes and fishing gear could've belonged to anyone."

Murph tooted the horn twice.

"After you." I held out my arm.

Detective Fay and Sergeant Will clambered back on board, and Frances followed me and retrieved the ladder.

The engine sound increased as we abandoned the birds to their human-free solitude.

Human-free, unless the council approved this hotel development.

I watched the island recede and reckoned I'd probably never land there again.

Frances and I helped pack up, as Murph and David fetched the tractor and trailer to retrieve the rescue vessel from the water. The police departed immediately, presumably to analyse the items they'd removed from the island. Maybe they were looking for Bozidar Radic's DNA?

"What were you doing on the rocks?" asked Murph, once we'd returned the boat to the shed, and the kettle boiled. "You had no reason to be up there. Safety first. You might've fallen."

"We were perfectly safe," said Frances. "I wanted to photograph puffins."

"You risked your necks for pictures of stupid animals that look like clowns?"

"They're endangered," said Frances. "Look at this one." She thrust a close-up of a waddly, orange-beaked bird at Murph, who brushed it away.

Frances showed the photo to me. "Shiraz likes them, don't you? Here, scroll through the pictures. There's a fantastic one of a nest."

I feigned interest and flicked through the images of the fluffy, triangular-beaked animals taken from different angles and at different zooms.

"I'll send them to you," said Frances. "Then you can have a better look."

"Um, sure. Ping me on Messenger."

I turned to David and decided to poke my nose into Emily's business. "Are you, um, going out with Emily tonight?"

"She said she'd meet me at the Smuggler's Tavern. My friends will be there too."

"Oh. Maybe she has the wrong end of the stick. I think she believed it'd be the two of you."

"Not on a Saturday night. Boys' night at the Tavern. The rugby's on the big screen. She'll love it."

I sighed and hoped Emily hadn't built her expectations too high.

"Emily, d'you like rugby?"

I'd skirted around the subject as I helped her get ready that evening. I didn't want her to know I'd asked David about their date. But I had to give her a clue as to what she was in for, right?

"I've watched the odd game at Redcliff Rugby Club. My dad used to referee for them. Why d'you ask?"

"I've heard there's an important match on tonight. The Smuggler's Tavern might be packed with rowdy supporters."

"We'll find a quiet corner. By the way, I took your silver dress up with my sewing machine as you suggested. D'you think I should wear it, or the white top with the red skirt? I can't decide."

"Um, maybe neither? Too formal for the pub. Especially with that sports crowd. Perhaps jeans, sneakers and a jumper?"

"No. I want to dress up like the other night. That was the first time a man's asked to buy me a drink since my teens. You don't understand, Shiraz. With your looks and fashion sense, men desire you all the time. I want to have men swooning over me too."

"Um, okay. The white top with the red skirt. And sneakers."

"Not sneakers. Could I borrow your wedges again? They give me an extra two inches."

"You're sure you won't be too dressy? I won't be with you this time."

Have it your way. But don't say I didn't warn you.

Emily prepared a late brunch for both of us the next morning, as I sat nursing a coffee from her dripolator. It wasn't a patch on the am-aaazing lattes from her café, but on Sunday mornings when the Wicked Whelk wasn't open, I politely allowed her to serve me a substandard caffeinated beverage.

"So how was last night?" I asked. "I didn't hear you come home. I fell asleep with my headphones on, listening to a true crime podcast. Now I'll have to start from the beginning to discover if the jilted ex-boyfriend killed her, or whether it was the handyman all along."

"Last night was a disaster." Emily slumped and shook her head. "An absolute disaster."

"Oh, no. What happened?" I stood and squeezed her arm. "Was the pub too busy? Couldn't you get a table in the restaurant?" I could see she was about to burst into tears. "Don't tell me he didn't turn up?"

"I'm sure David turned up." She bit her lip. "But I didn't."

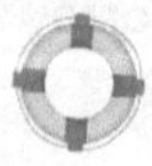

CHAPTER THIRTY-FOUR

"Emily, what d'you mean, you didn't turn up? I watched you leave the house."

She clonked down plates of creamy, fluffy scrambled eggs and crispy bacon on sourdough toast with a side of smashed avocado and red chili jam. "I walked to the pub and stared through the window. The condensation made it impossible to see clearly, but I could tell the place was packed. And that's when my heart rose in my chest, and I needed to sit down."

"Did you feel ill?"

"My head swam, and I thought I was about to faint. I sat on a bench overlooking the sea and tried to convince myself not to duck out. After several false starts, I told myself I was being silly. A couple leaving held the tavern door open for me, and I stared inside at the people drinking, chatting and enjoying themselves, and..."

"And...?" I prompted.

Emily hid her face behind her hair. "And I ran away."

"You ran away? You stood him up?"

"I texted him to say I didn't feel well. Crowds terrify me. I'm an introvert. I enjoy one-on-one conversation; a small number of people at most. When I saw all those pub-goers chatting and laughing together, I freaked."

"But you were fine with me last weekend?"

"If David accepts my apology, and ever gives me another chance, I'm going to drink half a bottle of Champagne with you first. This isn't me, Shiraz. I should stick to being a book-reading cat lover."

I wasn't sure how to respond to this, so I sipped my coffee and began to eat breakfast. Maybe I'd have to play matchmaker and arrange for her and David to meet privately? Which didn't seem right, as I'd once liked him myself. This whole Bozidar Radic affair had put me off men for now.

"A professional chef cooking for me is a luxury," I said. "On your day off, I should make brunch for you."

"Would that be wise?"

"Um, no. You're right. But we could ask Angela to cook us both brunch one Sunday?"

"I hardly like to ask her to do anything. She seems chirpy, but I'm sure she's tearing apart on the inside. She told me the police had taken Graham's computer away. I can't see why they'd do that?"

"Maybe he was involved in dodgy activities we know nothing about, and they hope something on the computer will lead to his killer?"

"Or maybe he was on Tinder, and the police are looking for contact details of secret lovers?" Emily sat back. "I know. Graham was having an affair with the mayor. He blackmailed her and said he'd expose their little dalliance unless she changed her vote to the 'no' side. So she murdered him to prevent their scheme from being exposed. Case closed."

"Um, that seems very fanciful. I can't imagine..."

KNOCK KNOCK KNOCK

We glanced at each other, grinned, and both said, 'Oscar!' Emily nipped down the stairs to open the door, and Cadbury tugged Oscar up the steps.

"Boots isn't here, is he?" was Oscar's first question.

"There's no way I'd allow Cadbury in if he was," said Emily. "He's probably sniffing around the fishing boats, hoping for scraps. Would you like a coffee? No, hang on, Earl Grey, no milk?"

Oscar laughed. "Is there anyone in Redcliff whose drink order you don't know? That'd be lovely, thanks."

Cadbury hoovered up leftover cat biscuits, as Oscar reached into his coat pocket and laid a small box on the table.

"Wow. You have a new phone," I said. "The latest iPhone. That's the one I want."

"It's very new and shiny, isn't it? My son met me at Headland Bay phone shop yesterday and helped me choose. And, I have a surprise for you. Close your eyes and hold out your hands."

I smiled, shut my eyes and resisted the temptation to peek through them.

I felt a weight in my palms. "This one's yours," he said.

I opened my eyes and gasped.

Oscar smiled. "The phone shop had a special offer if you bought two of the same model so I grabbed one for you. I hope it's the right colour."

"You picked this up for me? Really? Wow." I held the package and stared at the picture on the front. "It's perfect. How did you know I wanted pink?"

"A lucky guess. I'm sure you can take it back if it's wrong. You can send me the money later."

"I'm not taking this back. It's exactly what I wanted. Thank you so much." I laid it next to Oscar's phone. "How much do I owe you?"

"I'll have to look at the receipt. But it was much less than if we'd bought them separately. I presume you'll have to ring your provider and move your phone number across."

"Ooh," said Emily, as she set down Oscar's drink. "Where's my present?"

"It's not a present. Oscar collected it for me. I'm paying him back."

"Very nice," she said, lifting the box, turning it over and admiring it. "Now I'll have to upgrade too."

"My son helped me transfer the configuration," continued Oscar. "I'm not terribly good with technology, although I'm learning."

I confiscated my new toy from Emily and stroked it. "Phones become more complicated, don't they? I'll take some time tomorrow morning to set this up. And I'll need to buy a new case."

"Could you call my phone now, Emily?" asked Oscar. "I haven't heard it ring yet."

"Is it the same number?"

"Yes. The shop fixed that up."

She dialled, and the table vibrated to the sounds of AC/DC's 'Thunderstruck'.

Oscar pressed the 'end' button and clenched his teeth. "When my son said he'd transferred all the settings, I didn't realise he meant the ring tone too."

We laughed.

"We were talking about what the police might find on Graham's computer," I explained to Oscar. "Do you think there'll be anything?"

"I don't know." He removed a pad and paper from his pocket as if he were still a police officer on the beat, and I made a mental note to educate him how to take notes on his phone. "What do we really know about Graham? Who else did he come into contact with? Then there's Angela. Maybe she used the computer as well?"

"I can't see why she would've wanted her husband dead," said Emily.

"Who knows?" said Oscar. "Maybe they had financial problems. I can't imagine his shop brought in anything but a meagre income. Perhaps they argued about money, or maybe he had a life insurance policy that would pay out in her benefit? Or maybe she was having an affair? Anything's possible."

"She doesn't come across as someone who'd be unfaithful," I said.

"Maybe he was?" suggested Emily. "We wondered if the computer would reveal he was on Tinder."

Oscar shook his head. "All he was interested in was fishing and doing the best for Redcliff. He didn't seem an affair sort of chap."

"Perhaps he was away fishing so much, Angela grew to resent this and bopped him over the head. Case closed."

I smiled. "No one bopped him over the head, silly. He drowned. Do you have a photo of him, Oscar? I've realised that, apart from your description of a short, stocky man with unruly hair, I've never seen what Graham Woodhatch looked like."

"There's one on the council website. There are photos of all the councillors with soundbites about the miracles we expect to deliver."

"I'll look later." I nudged him and winked. "What miracles are you delivering, Oscar?"

"Apart from preventing this development of Blakey's Island, keeping the crime rate down, of course."

"Once a policeman, always a policeman?" said Emily.

We laughed.

"Talking about Graham's possible financial problems, I'll add 'unknown industry contacts' to our list of suspects," said Oscar, making notes on his pad. "Maybe he owed people money? Maybe he'd taken out a loan with someone and not repaid it? Maybe he was in dispute with an unscrupulous supplier?"

"Then there's still the mayor," I said. "They led opposite factions on the council; she was the head of the 'yes' vote, and he led the 'no' contingent. And you mentioned she might be taking bribes from the developers. Obviously she wants to see the hotel proposal go through so she can receive her backhanders. Could she have arranged for Graham to die?"

"That's an incredible theory," said Oscar. "I believe she's being dishonest, but that doesn't make her a killer."

"She has motive. Is there anyone else? We have four suspects, or groups of suspects."

"They're all flakey," said Emily, "apart from the developers. We have to investigate them. Presumably the police are already?"

Oscar nodded. "I know Johnny and his colleagues have all been interviewed. There's definitely motive. But the problem is, nothing places any of them near Redcliff at the time of the murder, except for Johnny. He was presenting to a public meeting which we all attended, so he has a perfect alibi."

I ran my hands through my hair. "We're missing something. I know we are. The clothes on Blakey's Island. The fishing gear removed from the boat. The 'B' carved in the victim's chest, as if the pirate had killed him. The expired cards in Graham's wallet. There's some big clue we've overlooked staring us in the face."

I didn't know it then, but the solution to everything lay on the table between us.

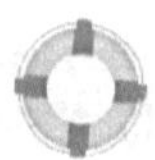

CHAPTER THIRTY-FIVE

Emily clumping down the stairs to the front door woke me briefly before six a.m., then I had a wonderfully magical three hours of sleep before noise from the harbour disturbed my dreams. My deepest sleep seemed to come after dawn, which was a major blocker for me ever being an effective café assistant, quite apart from my culinary ineptitude. Thank goodness for Angela; I could see how helping Emily plugged a gap in her life. Sitting at home gazing at the same four walls she'd shared with her husband would've been a torturous existence.

Shades of dark and light marched across the ceiling as the sun shone between patches of cloud. I drew back the curtains and stared out to sea. If I tiptoed and leant to my right, Blakey's Island came into view, beyond the harbour and the whitecaps whipped up by the strong south-westerly. A commercial trawler exited the harbour between the red and green lateral marks, bucking and riding the waves as it left the shelter of its anchorage.

There were two things I needed to do this morning. First, nip down to the Wicked Whelk and collect a takeaway. Second, bring the coffee back here and set up my new phone. It was a significant upgrade from my old one, and I wanted to save the unboxing experience until I had time alone. If you've ever owned an exciting, brand-new device, you'd understand my hesitation.

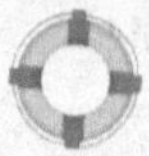

Angela seemed on edge as the coffee machine hissed and bubbled. Emily was busy in the kitchen behind her and gave me a quick wave over her shoulder. The breakfast rush was ending, and I presumed she prepared sandwiches and filled rolls for lunch.

"Sorry, Angela," I said. "I'm not very talkative until I've had my first coffee of the day. How are you feeling?"

"Horrible. I want this all to be over with. The police questioned me at length yesterday. I felt like they were accusing me of his murder. Me! We've been married thirty years, and granted, there's been many times when I've metaphorically felt like wringing his neck. But do they really think I'd be capable of murdering anyone, let alone my husband? Why don't they concentrate their efforts on the obvious killers? The hotel people."

"I'm so sorry you're going through this. An ex-police officer friend of mine told me, in any murder, the most likely suspect is always the partner, so this is standard procedure. All they want to do is rule you out."

"They're doing a lot of ruling out, then. This is the fourth time they've been in the house. I feel violated. They even pulled my furniture out from the walls and looked behind it. What they hoped to achieve by doing that, goodness only knows. Here's your coffee."

I took a sip, and Shiraz the gargoyle began to transform into Shiraz the human. "Have you had a busy morning?" I inquired.

"It's always busy on Mondays, because there's more prep for the week. Emily's asked me to work until closing time today. I wouldn't take any money from her; being at the café is infinitely preferable to watching those detectives tear the house apart."

"Of course it is. I must be going; I've a new toy to play with. See you tomorrow, maybe."

"Okay. Bye." Angela turned away and began loading the dishwasher.

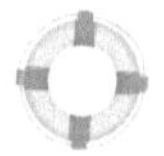

I prised open the phone's box. Even the cardboard felt top quality, and I was so happy I'd decided on the flagship. I wondered if Oscar felt the same, and whether he'd managed to change his ring tone yet. The new phone felt weighty in my hand, heavier than my old one. I slipped it out of the plastic protection. The screen had a peel-off cover, and I hesitated before removing it briskly and marvelling at the perfect, as-yet-unscratched glass. I was determined I'd look after this phone, and it would last me for years.

The power button was still in the same place as my old model, so I took a deep breath and pressed it. Once the familiar start-up sequence began, the manufacturer's logo appeared, and I smiled when I discovered the display seemed brighter than any I'd seen before. After skipping through questions asking for my details, I arrived at the home screen, and a message saying 'Emergency Calls Only,' because my SIM card laid at the bottom of the ocean, courtesy of Bozidar Radic. Wi-Fi from the Wicked Whelk was hit or miss, but the marine rescue station next door sent out a strong signal, so I connected to that and tested the Internet by browsing to Redcliff Council's website.

Under the section marked 'Your Council', formal photos of the members appeared, together with a one-line biography. Oscar smiled pleasantly from the page stating, as Redcliff's ex-sergeant and a former marine rescue skipper, he now enjoyed using his experience as a consultant to the police, keeping crime in Redcliff to a minimum. I smiled to myself, wondering if the current sergeant really appreciated his consulting, or whether he considered Oscar to be an interfering dinosaur. The mayor's picture announced how she was passionate about climate change, sustainability and supporting small businesses, as well as being committed to making Redcliff's facilities accessible for women, girls and people with a disability. Wonderful intentions, but she'd put so many catchphrases in one sentence, I wasn't sure how she'd have the time to save the world while taking backhanders from property developers.

The council hadn't yet updated the website to show the late Graham Woodhatch was no longer deputy mayor, and I stared at the face of a ruddy-cheeked, broad-shouldered, round-faced man with unruly hair, wearing a rumpled suit and tie which didn't sit well on him. The words under the picture stated his focus was promoting Redcliff's family holiday reputation and protecting the local fishing industry from the incursion of foreign trawlers.

The coffee I'd brought upstairs from the Wicked Whelk had gone cold, something I never permitted to happen. This new phone was really holding my attention. What next? Time to test the camera. I leant out of the window with the phone in my hand, stood on tiptoes and zoomed in on Blakey's Island.

Careful, Shiraz. Don't drop your new toy into the street on day one.

A quick few photos of the island to test the telephoto lens, and I drew my body back into my bedroom, gripping the phone as if my life depended on it. Next, I snapped pictures of boats bobbing in the harbour. The power of the lens amazed me; I could read the logo on a fishing crate at the far end of the harbour wall.

Cross-legged on my bed, I scrolled through the photos I'd taken. Enlarging the pictures with my forefingers revealed details I couldn't have seen with the naked eye, pulleys in the boats' rigging and lettering on their safety signs. I swiped right to the photos of Blakey's Island and inspected each one, zooming further in to discern individual bushes and rocks. The green paint of the hut poked through gaps in the foliage.

Then I came across a photo of a puffin.

Wow. Surely the zoom isn't that good?

I swiped to another picture with a group of puffins, and realised these must be the pictures Frances had sent me. Of course. When she messaged them to me, my phone was at the bottom of the sea, but now my new device had connected to wifi, they'd finally arrived from the ether. I scrolled and gawped at how clear they appeared on my new screen.

My eyes paused on the one she'd taken, when we'd scrambled up the goat-track path and looked down the rocks at the puffin's nests. Something didn't look right amongst the bushes.

I spread my forefingers.

I zoomed in as far as I could.

And there it was.

Definitely not right. Concealed amongst the bushes, with their face turned away, I discerned the outline of a human.

CHAPTER THIRTY-SIX

Murph stood at the wheel of the rescue boat which was tied against the harbour wall, departing imminently for sea training. On board were Frances and one other new recruit.

I sprinted from my front door. "Murph! Stop. Don't leave yet. Wait!" I leapt onto the vessel directly behind him.

"Hair-raising hydroplanes, Shiraz, you're not on duty today. What's the hollering about?"

"Look. Look at this."

"D'you have a new phone?" asked Frances. "Very nice."

"Not the phone. This picture. The one you took of the puffins. There's someone in it."

"Woah. Slow down," said Murph. "What's this photo of? What am I looking at?"

I zoomed out. "It's Blakey's Island. Frances snapped it while we were there on Saturday. Look at this." I zoomed in.

"We didn't realise at the time, but there's someone on the island in the bushes."

Murph took the phone from me, and I silently prayed his calloused hands wouldn't scratch the screen. "What d'you mean, there's someone on the island? It's a nature reserve. No-one's supposed to be there." He stared at the image. "Is it one of the police?"

"No. Both Sergeant Will and Detective Fay are tall and thin. Even though this figure's facing away from the camera, you can tell they're heavily built. They have a broad back."

Murph inspected the phone again. "When did you say this was taken?"

"On Saturday. When we ferried the police so they could inspect the warden's hut. Could we land on the island? Maybe this person needs help? Maybe they're injured?"

Murph puffed. "I've never landed on Blakey's Island during ten years of my career, and now I'm going for the third time in a week. We'll tell the Coastguard we have information there's someone on the island, and we're investigating. Frances, hop on the radio and advise them of our intentions."

I clenched my teeth and glanced left and right. "Um, could I come with you?"

Murph pushed the throttles forward, and the rescue boat departed the harbour. I introduced myself to the new recruit, a chap in his twenties called Justin, but I didn't have a chance to give him any backstory as to why I'd suddenly commandeered the vessel. The minute we left the protection of the sea wall, the southerly wind caught us, and we crashed across the waves. We all held on, as Blakey's Island appeared and disappeared between peaks and troughs of water. As Murph slowed off the island's northerly side, the rocks provided shelter and, within twenty minutes of leaving Redcliff, we were beaching.

"Frances," said Murph. "Take Shiraz with you and search for whoever's here. And be careful. Your safety comes before theirs. Don't go climbing any rocks. We can call for the Coastguard helicopter if they're in an inaccessible location."

"Right-o, skipper. We'll take the medical kit too. Like Shiraz said, in case they're injured. D'you remember your first aid training, Shiraz?"

"Um, yes. I've even had to put some of it into practice."

"Excellent. We'll be a good team."

We marched up the beach towards the warden's hut and the bushes. "Hello?" called Frances. "Anybody here? Hello?"

I swallowed, opened the hut door, cupped my hands around my mouth and yelled, "Marine Rescue. Is anyone here? Do you need help?"

Nothing.

I began to doubt myself, pulled my phone from my pocket and inspected the photo again. Definitely a person.

"Hello," yelled Frances. She turned to me. "There's no one here. Or if there is, they don't want to be found."

We stood in silence, gazing between gaps in the foliage. I turned around and saw Murph standing at the boat's wheel with binoculars to his eyes, scanning the island.

I'd almost convinced myself the blurry, zoomed-in image on my phone was a human-shaped rock, and I prepared for Murph's exclamations about how I'd wasted his time.

Then we heard a human-shaped noise.

"Did you hear that, Frances?"

"It sounded like a cough. A smoker's cough. Which direction did it come from?"

"In the bushes. This way." I parted the vegetation and headed for the right-hand side of the beach, towards the path Frances and I had climbed searching for puffins. In front of me, I heard rustling, as if a large animal was crashing through a jungle. "Hey, stop," I said. "We're marine rescue volunteers. We're here to help you. Stop! Why are you running away?" I put on as much speed as my yellow overalls and clumpy boots would allow, pushed through a dense lattice of shrubbery and met eyes with a man.

A short man.

A round-faced, broad-shouldered man.

A man who was supposed to be dead.

The man didn't seem injured or afraid, but he hung his head and edged away from me like a cornered animal.

"Graham?" I called. "Are you Graham?"

His reply surprised me.

"Am I? I don't know."

Frances caught up. "Is he hurt?" she asked.

"He ran away, so physically I think he's fine. But he seems confused." I called to the man again. "Come forward. We won't hurt you. We're here to help."

"Where am I?" said the man, staring around wide-eyed. "What day is it?"

"You're on Blakey's Island. It's Monday, and we're going to take you on a boat back to Redcliff."

"Where's Redcliff?"

"Not far. We'll be there soon. Come with us."

Frances radioed the boat. "Murph, we have one casualty. Male, middle-aged, not injured but unsure of where he is and who he is. He appears to be suffering from amnesia, or confusion."

"Can he walk?" asked Murph's voice.

"Definitely. He ran away from us."

"Escort him back to the boat. We'll assess further at base."

I turned to the man again, held out one arm and referred to him by his name. It felt strange to know this when he appeared to have forgotten it. "Graham. It's all right. Come with me. You're safe now."

Frances and I took an arm each, and our strange trio pushed through the bushes and walked down the beach. Graham glanced around as if this was the first time he'd seen the island, and he stumbled as we progressed.

"Jumping jackstays," said Murph, as we reached the boat. "Graham Woodhatch. I thought you were dead. Where've you been?"

"I don't know," said Graham. "Could I go home now?"

"Home to Angela?" I asked.

"Who's Angela?"

"Your wife. She's working in the Wicked Whelk café. She'll be so pleased to see you. Honestly, everyone thought you'd died."

Justin fitted a lifejacket onto Graham, and Murph reversed the rescue vessel away from the beach. Graham stared straight ahead the entire journey, his face devoid of emotion.

Frances radioed the Coastguard to inform them we'd rescued one male from Blakey's Island, who we believed to be the fisherman missing for over two weeks. They responded to state they'd contact the police.

I frowned, closed my eyes and turned something over in my mind.

If this man was Graham Woodhatch, whose body had Oscar identified?

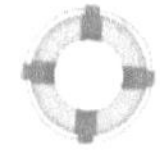

CHAPTER THIRTY-SEVEN

Graham sat on the couch at Redcliff Marine Rescue between Sergeant Will and Detective Fay. I perched on a chair and stared at him. Murph, Frances and Justin packed the boat's equipment away in the shed behind us.

Graham smelt.

Smelt like someone who hadn't bathed in weeks. Leaves poked out of his matted hair. Mud smears decorated his face, and his clothes looked like he'd slept in them. Which wasn't surprising, because he had.

"Where've you been, Graham?" asked Sergeant Will. "Spill the beans. Marine Rescue found your boat drifting off Blakey's Island two weeks ago. We discovered clothes and fishing gear in the warden's hut, where it appears you've been living. What's been going on, exactly? Because someone's died, and it's clearly not you."

Graham remained silent, with his hands clasped on his knees. He found the floor tiles fascinating.

"How did you survive falling in the water?" asked Detective Fay. "Did you swim to shore and stay on the island by yourself until someone rescued you? It's a good job you had the hut to sleep in."

Graham continued to say nothing.

"Look at me," I said. He raised his head and met my eyes. "Have you seen me before?"

He shook his head and shrugged.

"We were on the island together last Thursday."

Graham stiffened, and he bit his lip so hard a drop of blood appeared.

"Graham, does the name Anthony Blakey mean anything to you?"

His complexion turned white, and sweat glistened on his forehead.

Sergeant Will pulled out a notepad. "Start from the beginning, Graham. Tell us everything."

"D'you need me?" I asked. "There's someone I have to talk to. Right now."

Emily was turning the Wicked Whelk's sign around to say 'closed' as I threw the door open. "Hi, Shiraz," she said. "Is everything okay?"

"No. Everything is not okay. Where's Angela?"

"She's putting the rubbish out. Why?"

"Sit down, Emily. We need to talk to her."

"Why? What's going on?"

"I can't tell you. I need to see her reaction and compare it to yours. It's better if what I have to say comes as a complete surprise to both of you."

"You're not making any sense."

"Nothing's making any sense. Here she is." I called to her. "Angela, could we have a chat for a minute?"

"What's up, love? D'you need more tips on making sandwiches? I could share a few kitchen secrets."

"Sharing secrets, Angela, is exactly what I want you to do. Sit here with Emily."

They sat on one side of a table. I faced them as if I were in a job interview. Emily seemed genuinely puzzled, which is what I would've envisioned. Angela, I couldn't read so well, but her expression wasn't the same as Emily's. Trepidation, I would've called it.

"Angela," I said. "I have some wonderful news."

"Oh?" she said. Emily continued to stare at me as if my brain had flown away.

Deep breath, Shiraz. You'd better be right about this. Here goes.

"Your husband, Graham, turned up alive this morning on Blakey's Island."

Emily's eyes widened. She gasped, sat up straight and covered her mouth.

Shock. Exactly as expected.

Angela's face turned ashen, and she broke out in a cold sweat. Her eyes stared through me, and her body trembled.

Fear. Also exactly as expected.

"Did you know I'd say that, Angela?" I leant forward and met eyes with her. "You knew Graham was alive, didn't you? You might be a member of the Redcliff Amateur Dramatic Society, but this drama's well beyond your acting ability."

Angela covered her face with her hands and howled. Emily puffed out loudly and mouthed, "Shall I make tea?"

"Coffee, please," I mouthed back, as the wail of Angela's anguish echoed around the walls.

I clapped slowly. "A fantastic performance. The apex of your career. The grieving widow. Except, your performance wasn't quite good enough, was it? Once or twice, you let it slip you'd spoken to Graham since he"—I made air quotes with my fingers—"passed away. I excused them as emotional mistakes. But now I know differently."

Angela clawed her hands down her cheeks and exposed a face which had aged ten years in ten minutes.

"We didn't mean to," she said, a tear running down one cheek.

"Didn't mean to what? What have you done?"

I allowed her a minute to breathe, compose herself and almost definitely to decide how many beans she was going to spill.

"It was his idea," she said, finally.

"Whose?"

"That Blakey man. Anthony Blakey."

"You both knew Anthony Blakey?"

"Yes. And no. He rang Graham out of the blue and said he'd discovered his name on the Redcliff local history website as being the last warden of Blakey's Island. The website explained how passionate Graham was about the nature reserve. This was true. Graham would've done anything to protect the island." Emily brought tea, and I sat further forward.

"Go on," I said.

"He told Graham a story over the phone about how he was descended from the pirate two hundred years ago."

Her voice trembled. "He came down to Redcliff and met both of us. A very secretive man, was Mr Blakey. Our meeting was quite clandestine. He offered Graham his old job back and explained we'd be partners. Partners in a scheme which, he guaranteed, would prevent the hotel development. Graham was absolutely hooked, and I watched his spirits rise instantly. Although he loved running the fishing shop, it didn't bring in anything more than a meagre income, and the opportunity to return to the island and his old warden's position was an offer he couldn't refuse. Here was this smooth, suave city gent, who showed us his credentials, his documents with his name on them. An heir of the fabled Thomas Blakey, no less. But here was something I found ironic. It made me laugh inside. This famous pirate's descendant knew nothing about his own island, and nothing about boats. He'd never been in one. He needed Graham to help him take possession of the island and stake his claim."

Angela sighed. "Then he let slip the big secret. The one which, as we sit here, I wish we'd never heard in our lives."

She sipped tea, and I rotated my hands in a 'please continue' motion.

"Yes, indeed," said Angela. "The real secret of Blakey's Island. The story of the buried treasure."

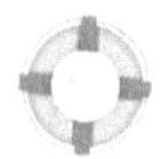

CHAPTER THIRTY-EIGHT

"Buried treasure?" Emily gasped. "So Jim Turner's pirate story has truth in it."

"Yep," continued Angela. "Legend has it, Thomas Blakey wrecked a ship full of treasure, and buried the spoils on the island. But nobody knew exactly where. Anthony Blakey suggested if Graham stayed on the island, refurbished the old hut and searched for the treasure, we could go halves. He'd keep half the treasure, as the owner of the land, and we could keep the other half."

"And you fell for that story?" I said.

"Hook, line and sinker, to use one of Graham's fishing terms. All our lives, we've been honest people. Never even had a speeding ticket. And where has it got us? Nowhere. Graham spends his days scratching a living from the business; we'll never be able to retire, and we'll be stuck here in this town forever. Maybe we're naïve; definitely gullible, but when this Anthony Blakey came to us with his proposal, we couldn't resist. He wanted to find the treasure and claim it for his own, but he needed Graham, his boat and his knowledge of Blakey's Island to help him find it."

"So why the disappearance?" I crossed my arms. "Why did he pretend to have died?"

Angela shook her head. "If we'd suddenly come into a fortune from this treasure, people would've been suspicious. We wouldn't have been able to enjoy the money. It probably wasn't Anthony Blakey's treasure, anyway. Even though he owned the island, the government would've seized it, considering the circumstances under which his ancestor Thomas Blakey gained it. We needed to come up with a plan to benefit from the treasure with no one knowing."

Emily watched, eyes wide, as Angela continued.

"Then, one evening, we were watching TV, and this programme came on about a man who faked his own death. He pretended to die in a canoeing accident to claim life insurance. He and his wife conned the insurance companies out of a small fortune and went to live overseas under false identities. Graham proposed we could copy their scheme. He even bought the book: *Out of my Depth*, by Anne Darwin. We got the idea from it, if Graham was ever caught, he'd feign amnesia."

"I see. Instead of defrauding an insurance company, you'd be defrauding the government."

"Exactly," said Angela, a morsel of excitement returning to her eyes. "If the rest of the town had found out about the treasure, we'd never have been allowed to keep it. So we studied the book and arranged Graham would fake his disappearance. He beached his boat on Blakey's Island, removed his clothes and fishing gear from it and pushed it off, to be carried away by the wind and tide. He hated seeing it go; oh, how he loved that boat, but the thought that we'd be able to buy a bigger one with the money from the treasure comforted him. And Anthony Blakey and us would both benefit from the discovery. He'd get his island and half the treasure, and Graham and I would disappear with our share to South America, where we'd change our identities and live like king and queen."

"I see one flaw in this plan," said Emily. "With Graham now marooned, and Anthony Blakey having no boating skills, how would you escape with your loot?"

"Anthony Blakey came to Redcliff again, and we told him Graham had to disappear for the scheme to work. He didn't like the idea, because it would have the police crawling over the island looking for Graham. But we stood our ground. So Anthony bought an old rowing tender from a man called Jim Turner. Graham fixed a small outboard motor to the stern and taught him the basics of using it."

"Lightbulb moment," said Emily, staring at me. "The tender said *Ruth* on the stern. Jim Turner's boat's called *The Anstruther Pirate*. *Ruth* must've been all that was left from the original lettering. And there was us looking for a boat called *Ruth* which had lost its tender. It was staring us in the face all along."

"But, Angela," I said. "Whose body's in the morgue? Who did you murder, to make it look like Graham had died? That would seem to be a much bigger crime than everything else you've mentioned. I remember that canoe couple's story, and they didn't take anyone's life to cover up their crime."

"Hey, we didn't kill anyone. We're not murderers. That wasn't our idea. Graham was perfectly happy to disappear; no body to be found. But Anthony Blakey said we needed to prevent the law from combing the island and discovering what we were really up to. He was prepared to do anything to stop the police finding out about our little treasure hunt. And he said, if they found Graham's body, they'd abandon the search for him. We didn't know what this actually meant until after the fact."

"After the fact?" I asked.

Angela's voice became quiet, and I strained to hear her. "Blakey scoured the London streets for rough sleepers until he found a vagrant who resembled Graham. He told us he drowned the poor chap in the River Thames, somehow made him unrecognisable and brought his body to Redcliff in a packing case on wheels. He dumped the body on the beach at night and left it there as if it was Graham washed up in the storm. He even asked us for Graham's jacket, phone and a wallet to make it realistic. We gave him an old phone and an old wallet with expired cards. He told us, with some pride, he'd carved a 'B' in the poor chap's chest, as some kind of homage to his pirate ancestor. We realised at that point Anthony Blakey was an unstable, dangerous man, and we haven't spoken since."

She took a deep breath. "Graham's been hiding on that island, living on canned food, searching for that stupid treasure, terrified that Anthony Blakey will return and kill him for real. Then he would've been murdered twice." She laughed, but there was no mirth in her expression. "Thank goodness for his mobile phone and solar charger. We talk every day, and I know he hasn't found any treasure yet. And I suppose, now he's caught, he won't ever find it, and we'll never be rich." She shut her eyes, covered her mouth and howled.

I tapped her shoulder. "There was no treasure, Angela. It was all a fairy story. Graham and you were pawns in Anthony Blakey's plan. He needed Graham to refurbish the hut and help him prepare the island as a prison. I was the treasure. Anthony Blakey needed you to get to me."

"Get to you?" she asked. "How's a marine rescue volunteer involved with this?"

"You've both been completely duped. There never was a descendant of Thomas Blakey. Anthony Blakey's real name is Bozidar Radic. He's been arrested for stalking and kidnapping me. When Jim Turner told me he'd sold his tender to a man called Radish, he meant Radic."

Angela gasped, and her complexion whitened. She gripped her face in her hands and wailed again. Emily and I looked at each other, our mouths in straight lines.

Angela raised her head. Her eyes were red-raw. "We're honest folk, Graham and me. We became tangled up over our heads in this, and we invented more lies to explain the lies we'd already told. We've been terribly, terribly stupid, haven't we?"

"Stupid?" I said. "Much more than stupid. You're both an accessory to murder, you've committed fraud, trespass, wasting emergency services' time, the list goes on."

"No!" wailed Angela. "Nothing was supposed to happen like this. All Graham ever wanted was to protect the nature reserve and prevent the hotel development. I wish, I wish, I wish we'd never heard of Anthony Blakey. Mr Radish. Whatever he's called."

"He's spent time in prison for stalking me; he followed me everywhere when I lived in the city," I continued. "And once he discovered I was living in Redcliff, he hatched this elaborate plan to create an island prison and incarcerate me there."

"Were you the girl he brought there two nights ago? Graham told me about that. He stayed hidden in case you saw him."

"That was me. Bozidar Radic needed a genuine reason to be in Redcliff. Without you, and your 'no' vote, his real motives might've been obvious. But then his plans got out of hand. He murdered that poor vagrant to keep the police fully occupied and throw them off the scent of his real reason— my kidnapping. By that time, you were both in too deep. You're right; Bozidar Radic would've killed Graham once he'd served his purpose. Probably you as well. Thankfully, he's in custody for the kidnapping, and I'm sure the police will be delighted to hear about all his other crimes."

KNOCK KNOCK KNOCK

"Oscar?" I asked. "Police knock?"

"It's not Oscar," said Emily, peering through the frosted glass. She stood and opened the door to Sergeant Will.

"I thought I'd find you here," he said, taking in the scene. "Graham's told us everything, Angela. I'll need you to come with me." He held out a pair of handcuffs.

Angela slumped, then looked at the police officer. "Before you take me away, could I please see my husband? We haven't met in the flesh for over two weeks."

"Absolutely not," said Sergeant Will. "If you're very lucky, you'll be in adjoining cells tonight, and you can shout bedtime stories to each other. I suspect you'll both be going to prison for several years."

CHAPTER THIRTY-NINE

"Whoever would've thought it?" asked Oscar. "Graham and Angela Woodhatch, both arrested. I feel sorry for them in many ways. Neither had previous convictions, and they were completely caught up in Anthony Blakey's web of deceit."

His hands circled a pint of beer, and Emily and I shared a bottle of Merlot as we sat around a table in the Smuggler's Tavern. Cadbury sighed from his position lying under us.

"And they were accessories to murder," said Emily. "Anthony Blakey completely fooled them."

I shrugged. "Me too, I'm ashamed to say."

Emily squeezed my shoulder. "From my perspective, it's very annoying to have lost my star café assistant. I suppose Angela will go to prison as some kind of accomplice."

"Who knows?" said Oscar. "She had knowledge of a murder and didn't report it. They both deceived people into thinking Graham was dead, and they definitely wasted police,

Coastguard and marine rescue time. But the real criminal's Bozidar Radic. The planning, depth and execution of his crimes was extraordinary. He went to the trouble of researching the pirate Thomas Blakey, legally changed his name so that he appeared to be a direct descendant, sought out poor, gullible Graham and inveigled him and his wife into his plan to construct an island prison. And all to abduct the woman he was obsessed with."

"Obsessed." I shook my head slowly. "My stomach churns thinking about it."

"Aren't you flattered, Shiraz?" asked Emily. "Someone would go to all this trouble for you? I wish I had a secret admirer. It would save all this dating business." She glanced around the tavern.

"Don't go there," I said. "I hope you're never stalked. Never wish for fame, ever. Oscar, with Graham in prison, where does this leave the hotel development? Are Johnny Chadwick's plans going through?"

"This," said Oscar mysteriously, "is where things get interesting. After Bozidar Radic was arrested, and the police exposed who he really was, I decided to research the pirate Thomas Blakey's family tree, and I visited the records office in Headland Bay. I wanted to convince myself that he didn't really have some useful descendant who could assist our resistance to the development, like we'd hoped the fake Anthony Blakey could. And here's what I discovered."

We crowded in to listen.

"The island was never legally the possession of Thomas Blakey. It was owned by his father, a man called Horatio Blakey, a trader who wasn't involved in smuggling or wrecking. Horatio had two sons by different women: Thomas, the pirate, and a second boy ten years younger, called Robert. Robert died when he was only twenty and, reading between the lines, I'd say his older half-brother murdered him. We know from history that Thomas Blakey wasn't immune to taking life, so it's no stretch of imagination to conclude he killed Robert. I suspect he did it to avoid sharing his father's inheritance, which included Blakey's Island."

"There was a lot of murder in those days, wasn't there?" said Emily.

"Yes, life was cheap," said Oscar, "and, as we know, Thomas Blakey continued his murderous campaign until he was eventually hanged for his crimes. However"—he held up one finger—"at the time of his death, his father, Horatio, was still alive."

"Hang on, back up," I said. "When Thomas Blakey was hanged, his brother, Robert, had been murdered by Thomas. So, with both sons dead, who inherited Blakey's Island when Horatio passed away?"

"Let's look forward one generation. Before Robert died by his half-brother's hand, he sired an illegitimate son, called John."

"Gosh," said Emily. "I think I can see where this is going. Horatio Blakey eventually died, and left his inheritance, including the island, to his grandson, John?"

"That's right," said Oscar. "Now, fast forward twenty or thirty years. John becomes a sailor and marries a local Redcliff girl. She's pregnant with their child when John himself is drowned at sea. At this point, his unborn son would logically inherit Blakey's Island, except John never left a will, and his wife didn't know about the island. Land records were sketchy in those days, and Blakey's Island eventually fell into public hands and became administered by Redcliff's local authority."

"What a shame. John's son probably died decades later, never knowing he should've owned the island."

"You've got it," said Oscar. "And his descendants weren't aware either. But now, thanks to the wonders of the Internet and my research, we can put that wrong to right. We can prove Horatio Blakey's family tree, stop the hotel development and return the island to its rightful inheritor at the same time."

"Wow. D'you know who that is?"

Oscar smiled and nodded. "I do. Rewind several generations. Horatio Blakey's grandson, John, never had the surname Blakey, probably because he was illegitimate. His mother gave him her name."

He paused, and his eyes twinkled.

"Go on," I said. "What was she called? Did you find it in the records?"

"I did," said Oscar, grinning. "Her name was Marion. Marion Turner."

Emily and I both gasped together.

"D'you mean…?" I said.

"Yep. To accompany his themed boat tour, Jim Turner's inherited his very own pirate island. Can you imagine how he'll dine out on being the great-great, however many greats, nephew of a real pirate? He'll never permit a hotel to be built there. The legend's worth more to him than any amount of money."

"Goodness? So the island's safe from development? I can't believe the mayor will be happy about that. Her Australian holiday, courtesy of the developers, just went down the plughole."

"That's another piece of news. The mayor will step down, as of today, and we can expect an announcement on social media and in the local paper. The council ombudsman discovered this isn't the first conflict of interest she's failed to declare, and she's been advised to resign before there's a public scandal. So the position of mayor is currently vacant."

"What does that mean for the vote?"

"Setting aside the matter of the island's legal ownership, as Jim Turner's claim will take some time to finalise, the council currently has eight members, as the mayor and deputy mayor are both, um, indisposed. One person's abstained, three are in favour, and three against."

"That's seven," said Emily. "Who has the mayor's casting vote in her absence?"

Oscar's smile reached the edges of his face, and he winked. "That would be the acting mayor."

"Oscar! Really? And you're still voting 'no', obviously?"

"Shiraz, we may've only known each other a few weeks, but d'you think after a murder, a kidnapping and being thrown overboard I'd change my position because I've been promoted?"

"What would Jim Turner say? Honest pirate?"

Oscar gave a thumbs-up. "Honest pirate."

We clinked our drinks together and laughed.

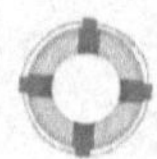

CHAPTER FORTY

The commercial fishing vessels, tourist day trip boats and pleasure craft bobbed and swayed in the harbour as I took my habitual morning stroll, my hot, steaming, double shot, skinny latte clasped between my palms. Emily was rushed off her feet today without Angela, although she'd declined my offer to help prepare food and drinks. Maybe she'd permit me to take the bins out later? That was hopefully within my culinary capabilities.

Jim Turner's boat rocked gently against the harbour wall.

"Morning, Jim." I waved. "Are you preparing for the Easter holiday rush?"

"Ahoy there. Arrr, t'will be busy enough in the coming weeks. Um, I have some booty that might belong to one of your hearty mates." He reached into a locker on his boat and handed me a battered, misshapen garment.

"Gosh, Oscar's trilby." I took it from him. "He'll be delighted to have this back. Where d'you find it?"

"Pulled it out o' the briney deep in my net, I did. Rescued it from Davy Jones. I'm hoping the seadog'll give me a few doubloons for it."

I laughed. "I'm sure he will. Thank you."

"D'you like my new sign?" asked Jim.

He pointed to a newly painted advertising board, and I read the text under the skull and crossbones at the top.

GENUINE PIRATE FISHING TRIPS.
BOARD A PIRATE SHIP.
MEET A DESCENDANT OF A REAL PIRATE.
HEAR THE STORY OF HIS PIRATE ISLAND.
LEARN ABOUT REDCLIFF'S PIRATE HISTORY.

I laughed. "D'you think you've mentioned the word 'pirate' enough? Congratulations on your new acquisition."

"Arr," said Jim, "Honest pirate. The sailors of Redcliff should take care in these waters. Pirates abound." He winked and continued with his preparations.

At the end of the harbour wall, I sat on the bench and stared out to sea. I leant forward to glimpse Blakey's Island to my right. My insides tingled knowing the nature reserve would now belong to Jim Turner, and the puffin birds and pirate legends could co-exist in peace.

I shuffled my bottom around and gazed back at Redcliff, the quaint little town that'd become my bolt hole from my unfulfilling city existence. My city existence which had followed me here, and I hoped it never would again.

The sea breeze blew my hair across my face, and I swept it back with one hand. On the opposite side of the harbour, I watched as the roller doors at Redcliff Marine Rescue opened, and a distant, burly figure with Murph's tall, broad outline entered. I clasped my fists and grinned at the thought of my next boat duty this coming weekend.

Redcliff-upon-Sea, with all its quirks and characters, was rapidly becoming my home. If only these murder mysteries would stop, it'd be perfect.

Although had I begun to enjoy solving them?

Shiraz's adventures continue in book 3: A Landslide, a Bride and a Fatal Ride.

SHIRAZ'S NEXT ADVENTURE

Hi, it's Simon.

Thank you so much for reading *A Deadly Affair in the Pirate's Lair*, the second in my *Shiraz Jones Marine Rescue Mysteries* series.

If you'd like to read more of Shiraz's adventures in Redcliff, why not:

Sign up for my newsletter at simonmichaelprior.com

Follow me on Amazon to be notified of new releases.

And please consider leaving a review to let other readers know how much you enjoyed it. A few words will suffice. Even if you didn't buy the book from Amazon, you can still leave a review there if you have a valid Amazon account. I read every one with interest and gratitude.

Now, if you wish, you could continue directly onto *Shiraz Jones Marine Rescue Mysteries* book three:

A Landslide, A Bride and a Fatal Ride

Available from Amazon and all good bookshops.

MORE BOOKS BY SIMON

<u>Available on Amazon and from all good bookshops</u>

<u>Shiraz Jones Marine Rescue Mysteries</u>

A Murderous Clamour at Redcliff Manor

A Deadly Affair in the Pirate's Lair

A Landslide, a Bride and a Fatal Ride

<u>Fun Travel Memoirs</u>

The Coconut Wireless:
A Travel Adventure in Search of the Queen of Tonga

The Scenicland Radio:
A Travel Adventure in Search of the New Zealand Experience

The Pomegranate Busker:
A Travel Adventure in Search of New Zealand Rock Stardom

The Anticlockwise Proposal:
A Travel Adventure Around the World in Eighty Diamonds

A Capybara for Christmas:
European Travel, Japanese Adventure, Maximum Mayhem

<u>Historical Memoirs</u>

An Englishman in New York:
The Memoirs of John Miskin Prior 1948-1949

DISCLAIMER

A Deadly Affair in the Pirate's Lair is a work of fiction, based on the experiences of Simon Michael Prior, a search-and-rescue skipper with one of the many volunteer marine rescue organisations seafarers depend on.

Although the book is set in England, the town of Redcliff-upon-Sea and the surrounding locations are fictional. Redcliff Marine Rescue is a fictional organisation. Montague Jones PR Ltd is a fictional company. Chadwick-Mappin International Hotels is a fictional company. *Red Carpet Superstars* magazine is a fictional publication. Which is a shame, as it sounds like a good read.

Names, characters, places and incidents are either products of the author's imagination or are used fictitiously. Any resemblance to actual events or locales or persons, living or dead, is entirely coincidental.

I had to say that.

ACKNOWLEDGEMENTS

This book wouldn't have been possible without the help of the following people: The wonderful beta readers: Alyson Sheldrake, Dawne Archer, Lisa Rose Wright, Louise Pierce, Rebecca Hislop and Val Poore; your feedback improved the final result so much.

Thank you to Victoria Twead, Matthew J Holmes, Meg LaTorre, Craig Martelle, Angela Ackerman, Becca Puglisi, David Gaughran and Dave Chesson for informative courses, tips and useful tools.

Thank you to Jeff Bezos, for giving independent authors a platform on which to publish our writing.

And thank you so much to the skippers and crew of the AVCGA Volunteer Coastguard. I couldn't have done it without you.

ABOUT THE AUTHOR

Simon Michael Prior experiences constant adventures, hazards and exciting situations as a marine rescue skipper and a commander of rescue operations.

Although Simon is absolutely nothing like Murph, Redcliff Marine Rescue's burly, grumpy coxswain, many of the scenes in his stories are inspired by events he encounters during his duties.

Simon has also lived on two boats and sunk one of them; sold houses, street signs, Indian food and paper bags for a living; visited almost fifty countries and lived in three; qualified as a scuba diving instructor; nearly killed himself learning to wakeboard and built his own house without the benefit of an instruction manual.

He now lives in it by the sea with his wife and twin daughters, where he spends his time regurgitating his experiences on paper before he has so many more that he forgets them.

Website and newsletter sign up: simonmichaelprior.com
Email: simon@simonmichaelprior.com
Facebook: @simonmichaelprior
Instagram: @simonmichaelprior

www.ingramcontent.com/pod-product-compliance
Lightning Source LLC
Chambersburg PA
CBHW030526120726
47904CB00005B/1646